For Edna :

" CLASS OF '54 "

DON'T TALK TO STRANGERS

Enjoy !

Amy Hook

Revised Edition 2012
ISBN-13: 978-1478371816
ISBN-10: 1478371811

"At long last, a crime writer who knows his stuff. Jerry Hooten is the real deal" James Swain, bestselling author of "Mr. Lucky"

"Jerry Hooten is a natural-born story teller." Michael Connelly, bestselling author of "The Lincoln Lawyer"

CHAPTER 1

Roger Wardlow was unhappy. That wasn't unusual, except he was even more so this day. He had received a notice of termination at the bank where he worked. Just as his mother would have said, "One more straw on the camels back." She had always had a saying for everything. He was starting his last week at the bank Monday. This was Saturday, and his day to work the drive-up window.

Marian had screwed up his breakfast again. The coffee was lukewarm, and the yolks of his eggs were runny. To top it all off, the toast was cold. No more than she had to do, you'd think she could get breakfast right. He checked the Timex on his wrist. It was about time to leave for work. He looked at the Timex again, another thing he'd had to give up, his Rolex.

Roger ignored her rambling on about her upcoming day. She was always griping about something. Maybe she'd get to the dishes stacked by the sink. He read the paper and choked down his breakfast. Marian was avoiding the topic of his dismissal at the bank. They usually wound up arguing when it came up. His supervisor, Barbara, was a friend of Marians.

He finished his breakfast and got his trench coat and hat from the closet. He walked out of the apartment with a mumbled "good-bye" to Marian. It was a strain for them to be civil to each other anymore. It was cold and rainy out today. Nearly spring in Des Moines was still wintry.

The old Volkswagen beetle sat forlorn in the parking lot. It fit right in with all of the other beat-up cars there. He ground the starter until it finally coughed to life.

Fate hadn't been kind to Roger. He had married Marian when she discovered she was pregnant. They had met in college and although Roger wasn't very impressed with her, he had married her out of a sense of obligation and his mother's insistence that he "do the right thing." He was much younger then, and back in those days, that's what was done. A short time later, Marian fell from a ladder while hanging drapes, injured her back and had a miscarriage. After that, she was unable to have children. Roger felt he had been cheated, but he continued with the marriage as Marian's family was fairly well off, and Roger's family was not. Roger's parents were killed in a car wreck shortly after his marriage, leaving them more bills than anything else. When her parents died, Marian had to share her inheritance with her four brothers, and that didn't leave them a great deal. Not nearly what they had expected.

Still, Roger had done well early in life. He was a CPA and was fairly good at it. Even though he wasn't particularly handsome, he was very neat and dressed well. He looked like a CPA. Then things rather got out of hand. He made some bad investments in technology stocks. The company he had worked at for thirty years downsized, and Roger was let go at age 57. He had a long spell of unemployment and most of their savings had been used to live on. The Cadillac had been traded for a Ford, then the Ford for their present Volkswagen. The Rolex had gone to a pawnshop. The membership at the country club had not been renewed. They had to sell the house and move into an apartment.

Things were on a downhill slide when Roger finally had gotten a job through a friend of Marians. Marian's friend, Barbara, was the branch manager at their bank, and when an opening for a bank teller had come up, she hired Roger. Now another downsizing and Roger was on the way out at age 59. One week from today, and he was through. Again.

Marian had been unable to work for years due to the bad back injury she had received in the fall that caused the miscarriage. She usually didn't complain too much, but lately Roger had been even harder than usual to live with. They argued more and more each day. She had gotten lax in her housecleaning, and that annoyed Roger also.

This was Saturday, and Roger would be the only teller working today. Barbara would come in at noon and they would close the branch for the day. The only services offered on Saturday were the drive up window and the after hours depository and Roger would be there until they closed. He and Barbara would do the closing together.

Roger didn't care much for Barbara. He felt that he had more knowledge than she and after all, he had his CPA. Besides that, Barbara liked to order him around and that rankled him. Marian always stood up for Barbara when he griped about her at home. They had been friends for years and belonged to the same book club.

The bank was giving Roger a going away party this coming Friday. He supposed he had to attend, but it made him furious to think of all the stupid employees that would be staying on while he was being let go. He didn't know if he could stand to listen to their half-hearted condolences. Why did everything have to happen to him?

CHAPTER 2

Business was slow. It was a cold, dreary day, and there was a cold draft coming in around the drive-up window. It was even worse when he had to run out the cage for a transaction. He didn't even make an attempt to be friendly to the customers in their warm cozy cars. They were a bunch of jerks anyway, too lazy to get their fat rear ends out of a car and do their banking during normal work hours.

The after hours deposit drop was dong a better business than Roger. It was the end of the month, and many of the area merchants were getting their accounts receivable. Roger had to go to the deposit drop twice just to collect the bank bags and move them up near the vault. When Barbara came in, they would put them in the vault for processing on the following Monday.

7

Finally, it was nearing noon and Barbara pulled into the employee parking area. She entered the bank, and went directly to her office. Roger closed and locked the drive-up window. He put the "Closed" sign in the window and turned off the little electric floor heater. He pulled the cash drawer out and took it to the desk to balance the account.

Barbara came out of her office and came over to his desk.

"How's it going, Roger?" she asked. She was reading an inter-office memo and didn't look up. She was dressed in sweats, another source of resentment for Roger. She couldn't even dress the part of bank manager.

Roger frowned at her, "Just peachy, for a short timer"

Barbara glanced up sharply at his tone. "Don't blame me, it's not my fault. If you had better customer relations, you might have survived this cut back. You and your attitude."

"What do you mean attitude?" Roger stormed, "I get tired of these jerks, whining about a missing penny, or the color of their checks. They think I'm here just to listen to them whine."

"Well, duh, you were, but you won't be much longer," Barbara retorted. "I feel sorry for Marian; she'll have to put up with you all day now."

Roger's lips were white with the effort to contain his fury. He turned his back on her and picked up his cash drawer. He was sick of this place. Time to get out; maybe stop at Toads for a drink before he went home to listen to Marian whine. He carried the cash drawer over to the vault and waited for Barbara to come over and open the vault door.

Barbara ignored him. She continued to read the memo, frowning at the sheet in her hand. Finally, she put it down and came over to the vault. Roger stood by impatiently, wanting to get it done and away from her.

She swung the door open. Roger had been looking away from her, unable to look her in the face. The vault door hit him sharply on the elbow, causing a jolt of pain to run up his arm.

Roger dropped his cash drawer, change rolling around the floor, and bills fluttering around.

"You stupid clumsy bitch!" he roared, all of the frustration and fury coming to a head. He swung at her with his other arm, nearly a reflex motion.

Barbara yelped and tried to step back, but she slipped on some of the coins rolling on the floor. Her feet came flying out from under her, and her head cracked against the edge of the vault door with a sickening crunch.

Roger stared in amazement. All of his fury and frustration replaced with fear. Barbara lay on the floor, her eyes staring at nothing. A pool of blood was quickly forming under her head, soaking some of the bills on the floor. She twitched a few times and lay still.

Roger knelt down beside her, careful not to get blood on his pants. She didn't appear to be breathing. He didn't want to touch her, but he gingerly felt for a pulse in her neck. Nothing there. He snapped his hand back. She didn't move. She was dead. Just like that. The stupid bitch had gotten herself killed!

Roger knew he'd be charged with murdering her; that was his first thought. It was no secret around the bank how they felt about each other, and most of the other employees took her side, the suck-ups. He had to get out of here.

Roger started running to the door in a panic. As he got his hand on the push bar, he stopped. He thought of what was going to happen. He didn't have a prayer. He'd spend the rest of his life behind bars, if he didn't get the chair. He'd lose what little he had left, at 59 years old.

He walked slowly back to the vault. Barbara hadn't moved, she still lay by the doorway, the puddle of blood still growing.

Wait a minute. All of those deposit bags. Some of those were big accounts!

Rogers mind was racing, there had to be over a hundred thousand dollars in those bags, sometimes nearly double that in a good month. He could get away. Hide.

He gathered up all of the bags and put them in a mail sack. He dumped the bills from his cash drawer in also. No use wiping away his fingerprints, everybody knew he was working this Saturday. With luck, nobody would find Barbara until Monday when the rest came to work. She wasn't married and lived alone. If he could get on the road, he could be far away before she was discovered. He would think of something, he knew he could.

CHAPTER 3

Far to the west, in a small town in Oregon, the chief of police sat at his desk and read the reports from the night shift. One domestic disturbance and one fight at one of the local bars. Big change from his days in L.A. He smiled as he remembered some of his nights on the force back then. "Oh yeah, big night in the wild west." he said aloud to himself, there was nobody else in the station. His dispatcher/receptionist had gone to the coffee shop for rolls and bagels.

He leaned back in the chair and frowned as he had another thought. The new chief of police in Los Angeles had sent him a letter inviting him to come back to the force. He was trying to rehire some of the old detectives as part of his program to upgrade the force and give it a better reputation. Some of his old friends had gone back, and they had also contacted him to try to persuade him to join them. The chief had extended the time frame for his return. The published time away from the force was three years. Because of Gary's record, and the fact that he had stayed in law enforcement gave him a break.

It had been five years since he had left the force and moved to Oregon. Five years since his marriage had gone down the toilet and nearly taken his law-enforcement career with it. The move had done him good, he got his head on straight and had managed to stay in law enforcement, even though on a smaller scale. He had made amends with his ex, although there was no chance of reconciliation. Neither wanted to get back together and his wife had remarried. His daughter had adjusted and they were all on good terms. His daughter visited him on a regular basis and they had a good relationship.

Now, he was seriously considering the move back to L.A. Not for the scenery, for sure.

14

He loved this part of the country, but he missed the challenge of his old job at homicide. He knew he'd come back here when he retired, it had too much of a hold on him now. He just felt he was missing a part of himself. He had some old ghosts to put to rest before he could be comfortable here. Part of his reason for leaving in the first place was the ghosts from his past.

He might have a problem being reinstated. Even though they had approached him, his five years here hadn't put a big strain on his investigative abilities. He needed a good solid case here that would prove that he could still cut the mustard. Nobody knew of his real reason for leaving the LAPD, it was something he carried with him in secret.

He looked at the reports again. No big case seemed to be hiding there. Something could happen, you never knew.

CHAPTER 4

Roger parked his old VW beetle in the apartment parking lot. He had put the mailbag in the back seat when he left the bank. He ran up the stairs to their second floor apartment. He hardly noticed the smelly stairway or the stains on the carpet. His hand shook as he tried to unlock the door.

Marian opened the door as he was struggling with the key.

"Roger, what's wrong? You look sick."

"Get out of the way, Marian, I've got to pack a bag and leave town for awhile." Roger pushed past her and headed for their bedroom.

"What in the world are you talking about?" Marian gasped, "Where are you going? Why?"

16

"There's been an accident, Barbara was hurt, and I'll be blamed for it," Roger twisted out of her way and pulled his small suitcase out of the closet.

"What do you mean? Barbara was hurt? What happened to Barbara? Is she all right?" Marian followed him around the bedroom as he grabbed some clothes and threw them in the suitcase.

He stopped packing and looked at her.

"She's dead, dammit." Roger shouted, "The bitch is dead. And I'm going to get charged with murder."

Marian stopped in her tracks.

"Oh Roger, what have you done?"

Marian stared at him. Her hands covered her mouth; only her eyes were looking at him, already convinced of his guilt.

Roger didn't move for a moment. Locked by her look. "It was an accident. I didn't mean to kill her. I mean, she slipped and killed herself."

Marian continued to look at him. He knew she thought he had murdered Barbara. Too bad, he didn't care what she thought; he had to get out of there. He closed the lid on the suitcase and turned to leave.

Marian grabbed at his arm, tears streaming down her face. "No, you can't just run away from this."

Roger pulled away. He wanted to throttle her. In all of their years together, he had never hit her, even though he had wanted to many times. He had always feared the consequences. Old habits died hard.

He opened the door and headed for the stairway, Marian right behind him. She reached him at the top of the stairs. "No, Roger, don't run. That won't help anything." She put her hand on his shoulder trying to pull him back.

Roger swung around to face her. His sudden move pulled her toward him. She tripped over the suitcase and went headfirst down the stairs, bouncing and rolling all the way to the concrete floor at the bottom. There was a loud snap as she slammed to a stop.

He stared after her in amazement and shock. His first thought for himself. "Not another one. I'll be blamed for this too."

He ran down the stairs, kneeling over Marian. Her head was twisted at a strange angle, her mouth slightly open, and her eyes still wet with tears and staring up at him, still with a lot of fear in them even as they dimmed. Two dead in less than an hour! Roger put down his suitcase, jumped up and pulled back. Emotions were mixed in him, fear, anger, remorse, and surprising him, relief. Strangely enough, he felt a sense of freedom.

The sounds of Marians fall had gone unnoticed in the noisy apartment house. There were no apartments here at the bottom of the stairway, and those at the top had the blare of TV's still coming through the doors.

Roger looked around; there was no sign of anyone. The parking lot was deserted of people. It was lunchtime on a Saturday; everyone was busy elsewhere. It wouldn't be long before someone discovered Marian at the bottom of the stairs.

His situation hadn't improved. He still had to get out of town, and fast. He grabbed his suitcase and ran out to the VW. He threw the case in the back seat with the mailbag and dropped into the driver's seat. After jabbing at the ignition, he finally got his shaking hands to insert the key and start the engine. He ground the gears into reverse and let out the clutch and backed out of his spot. He slammed the lever into first and roared out of the parking lot. He was on the run.

CHAPTER 5

It was Saturday night. Roger had driven to Omaha on I-80. It was the closest large city he came to when he started his run. He found a cheap motel on the north side of town. He put a phony name on the registration and paid cash for two nights in advance. The clerk couldn't have cared less; he hardly looked at Roger when he checked in, his attention on the TV program he was watching.

After checking into the motel, Roger drove to Eppley Airport and parked the VW on one of the top floors of the long term parking garage. With luck, it would be days before it was discovered. He went back to the terminal and caught a cab back to the motel. He had the driver drop him off at the office and carried his suitcase and the mailbag to his room. It was time to get a plan.

Roger sat at the desk, his head in his hands. Everything was going too fast. He had been operating on instinct ever since Barbara had taken the fall. He rose slowly and walked across the room. First Roger opened the mailbag and dumped the deposit bags on the bed. There were 27 of them. He used his pocketknife to open them and dumped the cash in a pile on the bed. He sorted the bills by denomination and counted the cash. The checks he would dump with the empty deposit bags and the mailbag. His eyes lit up as he surveyed the stacks of bills. This would be pretty good. He checked the lock on the door and began counting.

$175,890. All in unmarked bills. He scooped up the cash and tried to put it in his suitcase. He needed something to carry it in; there wasn't room in the suitcase for the money and his clothes. He had noticed a Wal-Mart down the street. There was a small bar next to it that served food. He would get another bag at Wal-Mart, and then get a bite to eat later. He had skipped lunch and was just now finding he had an appetite. He had to find a way to get out of Omaha. He was too close to home and when they eventually found the car at the airport here in Omaha, he wanted to be far away.

CHAPTER 6

Roger sat at a corner of the bar, eating his greasy cheeseburger and sipping on his rum and coke. This place was some kind of meat market for younger couples. It was a mixed crowd, mostly made up of singles. The tables around the bar were taken by those that had paired up. It was dark and noisy. He felt fairly comfortable here; no one paid him any notice. He was a little too old to attract the attention of the younger women. The bartender was busy enough not to bother him.

Roger hunched over his plate. After all of the running, his appetite had returned with a rush. There were several empty seats between him and the nearest customer. That suited him fine, he had to think. He had picked up a gym bag at Wal-Mart and stuffed the money into it. His bags were in his motel room, packed and ready to go. He had disposed of the empty bank bags and the mailbag in the dumpster by Wal-Mart. He just had to figure out a way out of town. Maybe a bus?

He had finished his sandwich and was nursing another drink when someone sat down next to him. Roger hadn't seen him come in. He wore a Wal-Mart vest and was about Roger's age. In fact, he bore a strong resemblance to Roger; slightly overweight, same color eyes and graying. His hair was cut short in a buzz cut, balding a little on top. The nametag on his vest said he was Richard Whiteman.

Richard ordered a seven-seven and looked around the bar, a little bleary eyed, finally looking at Roger. Roger tried to ignore him; he didn't need a conversation with a Wal-Mart greeter. Richard didn't notice a snub; he smiled at Roger and spoke.

"Hi, stranger, my name's Dick, what's yours?"

Roger didn't want to chat, but he didn't want to draw attention to himself either, he'd cut this short and get out of here. Dick had obviously had a few already.

"The name's Bob" Roger said, and turned back to his drink.

"Nice to meet you Bob. Haven't seen you around here before."

"Just passing through, thought I'd stop for one before I head back to the motel." Roger wished he hadn't ordered this last drink, he couldn't gulp it down, and he didn't want to attract attention by leaving a full drink on the bar. What was it his mother had always told him? "Don't talk to strangers." He smiled to himself.

"Where you headed, Bob? I'm hitting the road myself." Richard said, slightly slurring his words "I just finished my last night at Wal-Mart and I'm heading south for warmer country. I just stopped in here for a celebration drink before I hit the road. I plan on leaving tonight or tomorrow, be in Winslow, Arizona in a couple of days."

Now Roger started listening. This might be a way out of here. If he played his cards right.... "I was headed to Phoenix myself, but my old car died on me. Looks like I'm stuck until I can get me a set of wheels." He stuck a smile on his face and tried to look friendly: He wasn't sure how to do that; he hadn't had any practice for a long time, but like his mother always said, "Strike while the iron is hot."

"Oh, wow, that's too bad" Richard frowned, "Can they fix your car o.k?"

"Don't look like it, the mechanic said it was a cracked block. It was old anyway; he gave me a hundred for it for parts. I guess I was lucky to get anything for it."

Roger looked down at the bar, trying to look dejected. Now it was up to Richard. He could only hope. They had a few more drinks

27

and Roger was getting more information from Richard, information he might need if things worked out according to plan. He was also getting Richard more drinks and nursing his.

Roger told Richard a story of being down on his luck, low on finances. He said he had answered an ad for a job in Phoenix, and was supposed to have an interview. He only had a few days to get there, but he thought he could get the job. He didn't have money for a plane ticket, so he had to find another way to get there.

Roger kept the drinks coming, mostly to Richard, he sipped his own carefully.

Some time later, Richard was having a hard time with his speech.

"Say, you know what?" Richard said, leaning towards Roger, "I wouldn't mind having some company. That's a long drive to Arizona, and it's on your way. Maybe we could share expenses and driving. That would work for both of us. Whadda ya say, Bob?"

"Gee, that sounds great, but I just checked into the motel across the street. Think they'd give me my money back? I paid cash in advance. I've hardly been in the room. It would sure suit me if we could leave tonight, nothin' else is holding me here."

"That place? Sure. That guy that's the night clerk comes in here all the time. I'll bet he'd give you a break if we went over together and asked him."

Roger leaned over and grabbed Richard's hand and gave it a shake. "Sounds like a plan. Let me buy you that celebration drink." An hour and several drinks later, the newfound friends left the bar. Richard and Roger drove to the motel, with Roger at the wheel. Richard sat on the passenger side, looking bleary eyed out the window. They went into the office together, and as Richard had suggested, Roger got checked out by offering Fred, the night clerk, five bucks for a drink at the bar.

Roger went to his room and picked up his suitcase and the gym bag. He went back out to Richards Ford Explorer and put his bags in the back with Richards. Richard was out like a light, his head lying against the passenger window. Ten minutes later, they were on the 680 bypass, heading west. Richard had been staying at a motel also, and had already packed his belongings in the Explorer. He had told Roger that if he didn't leave that night, he was planning to leave first thing in the morning. He had nothing in the room and was already paid through the night. They didn't bother to go by his motel.

Richard and Roger had agreed earlier that it was better driving at night; less traffic and it moved faster. Roger couldn't believe his string of coincidences. His entire life had been turned around by violence. First bad luck, a double shot of it with Barbara and Marianne, now good luck, finding Richard. He was excited with this new break. Maybe things were going to go his way for a change. As his mother would have said, "All's well that ends well."

CHAPTER 7

Roger was starting to feel better. The robbery of the bank and the two dead women had been connected. According to the news, Roger was the prime suspect. Luckily, they didn't yet have a picture to go with the story. He had found a Sunday edition of the Des Moines Register at the truck stop in Lexington, Nebraska. The description they had would fit a lot of people, Richard included. In his favor, the police were looking for Roger traveling alone. There was no mention of finding the car and they didn't give a direction of travel. The bad news was that the FBI was involved. Bank robbery and possible interstate flight were mentioned in the article.

Roger drove until sunrise. Richard had slept through the stop for gas and coffee in Lexington. He held down the speed. He didn't want the troopers pulling him over. Richard woke up as they were leaving North Platte. He was surprisingly in pretty good condition after all he had drunk the night before. He was a little disoriented at first, he didn't remember being talked into leaving Omaha the night before. They stopped for breakfast and then Richard took the wheel. When Roger woke, they were in Colorado, heading southwest on I-25.

Richard talked while he drove. He told Roger about his wife, how she had died of cancer, the fact that they never had children and neither of them had any close relatives. Richard had been an over the road driver until his wife got cancer, and then he quit to stay with her. She hadn't lasted long. Now Richard had nothing to tie him to Omaha, and since he had spent years traveling across the country he decided he wanted to spend the rest of his life away from the Nebraska winters. He had his pension and Social Security to live on. Roger mostly listened. He had given Richard a story of losing his job and his wife and being alone for several years. Richard could relate to the story and swallowed it, hook, line, and sinker.

"I sold the old house when the wife got sick. It was too much to take care of the house and her both. We moved into an apartment until she passed on. I've been living in a motel the last few days, getting ready for this trip. I'm planning to get a room in Winslow until I find a place there to move into. I've already had my stuff shipped there. Didn't have too much, sold most of the furniture and household goods. My old company gave me a real break moving my goods for me." Richard sat in the passenger seat, looking out the window as though he was looking at his future.

As they traveled, Roger began making plans. He had nothing against Richard, but he had decided that he needed Richard's identity in order to disappear and start over. Their descriptions were very similar, and even though Richard was a few years older, he thought he could pass. He hoped he'd be able to do the job when the time came. He needed some kind of a plan and a chance to carry it out.

CHAPTER 8

The opportunity came the next day. They were driving somewhere in northern Arizona. They had turned off the interstate to take a short cut that Richard knew from his days on the road. It was a long desolate section of two-lane road. They had filled up with gas before embarking upon it, as there were no places to stop for over a hundred miles. About fifty miles in, the right front tire blew.

Roger was driving at the time. He was half asleep at the wheel when the tire went. It caught him off guard. The wheel pulled to the right, and they went off the pavement onto the shoulder of the road. They slid to a jerky stop and Richard was half thrown out of his seat. He had taken his seatbelt off while he napped. His head banged into the dash and he held on with both hands while they dragged to a stop. He had a small cut on his forehead that began to bleed down into his right eye.

Roger sat behind the wheel for a minute after they stopped. The blow out had shaken him. They had come to a stop on the shoulder of the road, the Explorer tilting to the right front.

"You all right?" he asked Richard, who was sitting against the door, still hanging onto the dash.

"Yeah, I'm o.k., just a little shook up." Richard had a trickle of blood flowing down his cheek.

They both got out together to take a look at the damage. The tire was twisted around the rim, the front bumper close to the ground. There was a big piece of glass sticking out of the sidewall.

"Going to be a bugger to get jacked up." Richard growled, leaning against the front fender.

"I'll get it," Roger said, "You sit still and put something on that cut."

Roger went to the back of the Explorer and opened the rear gate. The jack was lying on the floor behind the rear seat. He pulled out the jack handle and began removing the spare from its mount on the back of the Explorer. He rolled the spare to the front of the Explorer and tried to get the jack under the front bumper. He couldn't get it down low enough.

"Let me do that," Richard said, "That isn't the regular jack, the previous owner stole the original. That one's a Wal-Mart replacement."

Richard started digging a shallow hole under the bumper with the jack handle. After a lot of scraping and cursing, it was deep enough for the base of the jack, and low enough for the jack to get a purchase on the bumper.

"Your turn," Richard sat down on the ground in the shade of the car. He was sweating and puffing from the exertion. He handed Roger the jack handle. "I've had it."

Roger stood for a moment, turning the jack handle in his hands. He should do it now. The handle was slippery in his sweaty hands. He stood there, looking from the handle to Richard and back. The jack handle seemed heavy and ominous. He envisioned swinging the handle at Richards head. One swing. Smack! That's all it would take. He shuddered.

He couldn't do it. Barbara and Marian had been accidents. He was no killer.

"What's the matter, don't you know how to use one of those?" Richard grinned up at him.

Roger could only stare back at him. He took a staggering step back, then turned to the front of the car and started loosening the lug nuts on the flat tire. His mind was a whirl. He had to do this. It was his chance for a new life. His only chance.

He moved like a robot, jacking up the car, and changing the tire. His hands were shaking and he was soaked in a cold perspiration that had nothing to do with the desert heat.

Richard sat by the car the whole time, oblivious to the turmoil going on in Rogers mind. He was leaning against the side of the car, his eyes closed. It would be so easy. One hard swing with the jack handle.

He loaded the jack and the twisted flat tire into the back of the Explorer and slammed the lid closed. The jack handle was still in his hand. He looked at it like it was something he had never seen before.

"You ain't gonna steal my jack handle, are you?" Richard was at the rear of the Explorer, looking at Roger with a grin on his face.

Roger stared at him as though he were a stranger, the thoughts of murder still swirling through his brain.

Richard reached out and took the jack handle. He opened the back and dropped the handle in with the flat tire. He closed the lid and turned to Roger.

"I think I'd better drive for awhile, you don't look so good." Richard reached out and held Roger by his shoulder. He pushed him gently to the passenger side of the Explorer.

"Let's get moving." Richard opened the driver's door and sat in the seat, pulling his seatbelt on. Roger got in and fastened his, still not saying a word. He sat there, immobile, while Richard started the Explorer and pulled back onto the highway. The chance was gone; he was doomed.

All this time, not one other vehicle had passed from either direction. What a perfect spot. How had he messed this up? He'd never get another chance like that. Roger felt all of the whirling emotions settle into his stomach.

"Pull over Richard, I think I'm going to be sick."

Richard pulled to the side of the road. Roger fumbled off his seat belt and lurched out of the car, vomiting into the dirt at the side of the road. He leaned over, his hands on his knees, but he had still lost most of his breakfast on his shirt.

"Whoa dude, you going to be o.k?" Richard asked.

Roger just kept leaned over, unable to speak.

"It's the heat and the exertion" Richard said, "Just sit there in the seat awhile and get settled down. I'll grab another shirt for you."

Roger leaned back on the passenger seat, his feet on the ground outside of the car. Richard went to the back and opened the lid again. Roger sat still; his eyes closed and tried to pull himself together. Something would come up, he'd think of something.

CHAPTER 9

"What the hell is this?" Richard was standing in front of Roger, a wad of money in his fist. "Your little bag is full of this. I thought you were about broke. What are you, a bank robber?"

Richard had opened the wrong bag looking for a shirt for Roger. He glared at Roger, the blood from the cut over his eye smeared on the side of his face, giving him a grotesque look.

Roger looked up in dismay. "I can explain, it was an accident." he wailed, "I didn't mean for either of them to die." He was blubbering now, everything was going to pieces. He had come so close. Now it was all going to end.

Richard stared at him, uncomprehending. "What the hell are you talking about?" He stepped back away from Roger, his hand with the wad of money falling to his side.

"You kill somebody too?" He started backing away, a look of fear crossing his face.

"I can explain," Roger said, "It was all a mistake." He reached out to Richard, but Richard kept backing away, looking at him like he was a monster.

It always happens to me. Roger was beginning to get angry. Why me? Again?

He followed Richard, who was still backing away, the money forgotten in his hand.

Richard turned and began to run back down the highway. Roger started after him and slipped on his own puke on the ground. Richard was getting farther away. He had to stop him.

He started after him, but Richard was much faster and getting further away.

Roger turned back to the Explorer. The engine was still running. He put the car in gear and pulled a u-turn and started back for Richard.

Richard was running full out now in a panic. Roger bore down on him, anger taking over for him and energizing him again.

"Not this time." Roger shouted, "You can't do this to me."

He hit Richard in the back at 40 mph. Richards head snapped back and slammed on the hood, making a dent it where it hit. Roger slammed on the brakes and Richards body flew into the ditch along the side of the road. It rolled and flopped face down then lay motionless in the ditch.

Roger pulled up and got out of the car. Richard was starting to move. He was still alive. Roger froze. He edged back to the car, his eyes on Richard. He had pulled himself to his hands and knees, his head hanging down, blood dripping to the ground.

The back lid was still open from Richards untimely search for a shirt for Roger. Roger reached in and got the jack handle again. This time he could do it. He had to do it!

He approached Richard cautiously, as though afraid he would rise up and get him. He could see that Richard was hurt bad, the back of his head was a mass of blood. He walked around in front of him and raised the jack handle above his head.

Just then, Richard looked up, a mixture of pain and disbelief on his face. His eyes locked on Rogers, his mouth opened to speak.

Roger screamed in horror and brought the jack handle down with all of his strength. It hit Richard a glancing blow on the head and down to his shoulder. His arm collapsed and he fell face down to the dirt again.

47

Roger dropped to his knees and began raining blows on Richards head with the jack handle, screaming and crying at the same time.

When he finally focused his eyes and looked at Richard, he froze again. The back of Richards head was a mess of broken bone and gray bloody tissue. He didn't move anymore.

Roger rose to his feet and staggered back to the Explorer, throwing away the jack handle. He leaned against the side of the car, drawing in deep breaths, shuddering with each intake. He shook all over; his heart was pounding in his chest.

He leaned against the back of the car, looking down the road, to the mountains, anywhere but at Richard. He had done it. Maybe things would work out after all.

His eyes snapped back to the road. What was that? There was a black speck on the road heading his way. Somebody was coming.

CHAPTER 10

Quickly, Roger looked back at where Richard lay in the ditch. He could be seen from the road. He had to move now.

He ran back and rolled Richards body further into the ditch. If he could get the Explorer closer, he could block the view of the body from the road. He ran back and jumped in the drivers seat. A quick glance showed that the car was still just a speck in the distance, but growing larger. He yanked down the gear lever and pulled around again so that he was facing the right direction and blocking a view of Richard's body. As long as they didn't stop, the people in the oncoming car wouldn't see him lying there.

It had been half an hour since the blow out. In all that time, no car had come by. Why now? What if it was a state cop? What if they stopped?

The speck was growing larger. It looked like a pickup truck. At least it wasn't a cop. Roger decided to stay in the car behind the wheel. Maybe they'd just keep going.

It was getting closer. Traveling fast. That was good; maybe they were in a hurry.

As the truck came nearer, it began to slow down. NO! KEEP GOING! Roger screamed silently at the driver. No such luck, it was going to stop.

Roger rolled down the driver's side window and forced a smile on his stiff features. The driver of the pickup came to a stop and rolled his window down also.

"Everthin' o.k.?" a bearded man said, giving Roger a look through dark sunglasses.

"Just fine, just taking a break." Roger replied, trying to hold the man's eyes.

The man sat there for what seemed an eternity, smiling back at Roger.

"Okey Dokey, you have a nice day now." The man said, rolling up his window and starting to roll forward.

Roger sat staring at him, the smile still stuck on his face.

Suddenly, the truck stopped again and the window came back down.

"You got plenty of gas? It's still a fur piece to the Git n Go."

"I'm fine," Roger said, "Plenty of fuel. Thanks."

Another grin, and the driver looked forward, taking off again.

Roger sat there until the pickup was a speck again, going away.

He jumped out of the Explorer and back to the body of Richard. He couldn't leave it here, it would be found. The money was still clenched in Richard's hand. He pried the fingers open and jammed the bills in his pocket. Like his mother always said, "Waste not, want not." He rolled and dragged the body back to the car, then heaved it up into the space in the back. He went back and got the jack handle and threw it in with the body. He threw the luggage into the back seat and pushed the body deeper until he could close the latch again.

He got back in the drivers seat. He looked in both directions. No more specks on the highway. He sat there until he quit shaking, then started back down the road.

Half an hour later, another road bisected the highway. It was a two lane county road stretching off north and south of the main highway. Roger pulled to a stop and looked in both directions. To the north, the mountains dominated the horizon. To the south, nothing but flat desert. He turned right, heading to the mountains.

CHAPTER 11

The mountains seemed to move farther away as Roger drove towards them, the distance never seeming to lessen.

After thirty minutes of driving, Roger was in the foothills, driving higher. If possible, this road was even more deserted than the highway. There was no sign there had ever been anyone here before him.

The road got steeper and wound around in sharp hairpin turns. At times, there was a drop-off that was frightening in its closeness to the road. Around a turn and Roger saw a faded sign by the side of the road, "Scenic Lookout Ahead" and under that was a smaller sign stating, "1 Mile".

Roger slowed as he approached the pull off. He could see for miles. The drop off by the side of the road was sudden and steep. A rusted chain link fence set back from the edge with warning signs hanging from it. "Steep Drop Off, Stay Back".

Roger got as close to the edge as he dared, and looked down. Vertigo set in immediately. The drop off was spectacular. Far below, crags and crannies broke up the edge of the mountainside. This would be a perfect spot for Richards final resting place.

He went back to the road and peered in both directions. As he expected, there was no sign of any vehicles in either direction. There was no sound except for the ticking of the cooling engine of the Explorer and the wind blowing through the pine trees.

Roger opened the back of the Explorer. Richard's body lay twisted in the space behind the seat. He pulled the body to the edge of the truck and went through his pockets. He opened Richard's billfold and looked at the drivers license. Richards picture stared back at him, a

54

slight smile on his face. Close enough, he could pass. He checked the other cards in the billfold. There was a MasterCard, a Sam's card along with a Medicare card and a Blue Cross medical card.

There was a folded envelope in his other back pocket. In the envelope was a letter from the postmaster at Winslow, Arizona. It stated that his mail would be held at the general delivery window at the main post office in Winslow for his arrival.

Some change and a pocketknife was the remainder of Richard's belongings. Roger took them and put the whole works on the passenger seat of the Explorer. He thought about putting his billfold in place of Richard's, then discarded that idea. He would dispose of his identity later. No need to connect himself to another body.

He left Richard on the edge of the trunk and backed the Explorer closer to the edge of the drop off. He got out of the car and pulled Richards body over to the edge. He got as close as he dared and then sat on the ground and pushed Richard over the edge with his feet. He heard the body strike once, and then silence. He crawled over to the edge and peered down. There was no sign of the body anywhere. Hopefully, it had fallen into one of the deep crevices on the side of the mountain. It probably would go undiscovered for years.

He jumped back to his feet and closed up the Explorer. He got into the drivers seat and drove back down the mountain. He drove all the way back to the highway without seeing another car. There were no houses in this part of the desert either.

He pulled to the side of the road before getting on the highway. He pulled off his filthy shirt and wiped his face with the shirttail. He got a bottle of water out of the back seat and poured it over his head and hands. He wadded up the shirt and was going to throw it away when he thought better of it and stuck it into an empty plastic sack. No sense leaving any evidence that he had ever been here. He would dispose of it later.

He got back on the highway and started west again. A new sense of release came over Roger and he smiled as he drove across the empty desert.

CHAPTER 12

Roger checked into the Motel 6 in Winslow, Arizona as Richard Whiteman. His first use of his new identity. He still paid cash. He wasn't sure that he felt comfortable using the credit card yet. He dumped the bag with his filthy shirt in the motel dumpster. Later, he ate a quiet dinner at the Denny's across the street from the motel and slept soundly that night.

The following morning, he had breakfast at Denny's again and got directions to the main post office. He drove to the post office and parked in the customer lot. The post office was a typical government building, just like every other post office he had ever been in. He wasn't sure where General Delivery was, so he went to the counter and stood in line. The clerk smiled at him and informed him he was at general delivery. Roger gave him Richards name and asked if there was any mail for him.

The clerk walked over to a case adjoining the window and looked through the pigeonholes. He pulled out some mail and brought it back to the window.

"Here it is," said the clerk, "I'll need to see some identification."

Roger panicked. He hadn't thought about this. He had to try the driver's license. He pulled out Richard's billfold and removed the drivers' license with shaking hands. He dropped it on the counter in front of the clerk.

The clerk picked it up, still smiling, and looked at the license and then at Roger.

"Looks like you've let your hair grow out." He smiled. Then he handed the mail over without another word. He held the drivers license out for Roger, still smiling at him.

Roger just stared at him. Too shocked to move. It had worked.

The smile began to fade on the clerks face, "Sir, there are other customers waiting."

Roger shook himself back to reality. He tried a smile and reached out and got the drivers license back from the clerk, then picked up the mail and walked away from the counter.

He sat in the Explorer and took a deep breath. It worked. He would work on his appearance to make it look more like the picture of Richard on the license. No more surprises like that.

Roger picked up the mail and sorted through it. There was a letter from a storage facility with a highway address. In their conversations, Richard had told Roger he had shipped a few things ahead. He had mentioned that he had only driven through Winslow in his 18-wheeler and had dropped a shipment there for a customer. He had like the look of the town and always wanted to return. Roger felt safe that there would be no one that would know

Richard. Even at that, he would feel better moving on.

There was another letter from a Bank America branch in Winslow stating that his account had been transferred from the Bank America in Omaha, and his retirement check was being direct deposited to it. There was another from the MasterCard account, showing a small balance, a confirmation of his change of address, and a $5,000 credit line. The payment due date wasn't for another two weeks.

Roger drove to another motel, this time a Best Western, quite a bit nicer than the Motel 6 he had stayed at last night. He checked in this time using the credit card. He had practiced Richard's signature in the Explorer, using the signature on the drivers' license as a guide. The clerk checked him in with a smile, calling him Mr. Whiteman, and gave him a room key and directions.

Roger went into the room, taking everything from the Explorer. He emptied

Richards bag on the bed and went through it. The shirts would fit o.k. The pants were another matter. They were too small around the waist and too short in the inseam by about an inch. According to Richards drivers license, they were both the same height and Roger was about 10 pounds heavier.

Roger took the pants, and his billfold with all of his cards and identification and put them in the plastic waste bag from the room. He had noticed a trash room at the end of the hall. There was an incinerator there. He walked down to the trash room and threw the bag in the incinerator. He watched as his old life went up in flames. He went back to the room and sat at the desk practicing writing Richards name until he felt he could pass it off as his own.

He went into the bathroom and looked at his face in the mirror. He held the drivers license up and checked the differences. Richard's hair had been much shorter, but his bald spot didn't show in the photo. Roger decided to get his hair cut off short to help make them look more alike. Other than that, their appearance was close enough. Rogers' eyebrows were a little heavier, but he fixed that with his electric razor.

He put the clothes back in Richard's suitcase and decided to throw away his old one. It was just a cheap plastic job anyway. He dropped it in the trash room. Maybe someone else could use it.

He was ready to go to the bank for the final test.

CHAPTER 13

Roger drove over to the branch office of the bank. He had picked up a map of Winslow when he gassed up the Explorer and got directions to the address of the bank. After his episode at the post office, he had a new confidence in his ability to pull off the deception.

He stopped at a barbershop and got his hair buzzed off. As he paid the barber, he looked in the mirror behind the chair. The new Richard Whiteman looked back at him.

He drove into the parking lot and parked by the entrance to the bank. He checked to make sure he had the letter from the bank manager. He pushed into the lobby and walked to the counter. There were no other customers.

"Hi, I'm Richard Whiteman and I'm here to see about my account."

The young girl at the window looked at his letter and directed him to an office at the corner of the room.

"I'll call Mr. Patterson and tell him you're on your way." She said with a smile.

Roger walked back to the office. The door was open and a middle-aged man was sitting at the desk, the phone to his ear. He hung up the phone and motioned Roger into his office with a smile.

"Mr. Whiteman." He reached across his desk to shake Rogers hand. "How nice to meet you in person."

"My pleasure," said Roger. "I'm happy to be here."

"Everything is set up. I have your transfer records here, your ATM cards, and a checkbook, all ready for you."

Mr. Patterson pushed some papers across the desk. "If you'll just sign these, and let me see some I.D., we can have you set up and on your way in just a few minutes."

Roger pulled out his Richard Whiteman drivers' license and handed it across the desk. He took the pen offered to him by Patterson and sat at the chair with the papers.

"If you'll just sign here, and here, and here." Patterson pointed at the different spaces on the papers. "This top one is your checking account. I'll need you to verify the balance by initialing in the space next to it."

The checking account showed a balance of a little over $2,000. The savings had $25,000 in it. Roger had him transfer another $3,000 into the checking account. He felt more comfortable with access to more money through a check.

Roger followed Patterson's instructions, initialing by each balance, and signing each document.

Patterson handed him a folded piece of paper. "This is the P.I.N. number for your ATM card. With it, you'll have access to both your checking and savings from any ATM machine in the country."

Roger opened the paper and looked at the number. He folded it again and stuck it in his billfold.

"Oh, and here is your drivers license back." Patterson said, smiling and handing it over.

Roger gathered up his copies of the papers, and his checkbook and savings account book.

"Thank you for doing business with us Mr. Whiteman, we are proud that being a national bank, as we are, makes it easier for our customers to relocate. No muss, no fuss, no hassle. Let us know if there is anything further we can do to help. If you're interested in purchasing any property here, we'd be more than happy to have your business."

Roger shook hands again and left the bank. He couldn't believe how easy it had all been. Now he truly had a new identity, and some finances to back it up.

He drove back to the motel and went back into his room. He thought about settling here in Winslow. The winters would be mild, and nobody knew him here, either as Richard Whiteman or Roger Wardlow. The only problem was he didn't know if Richard had said anything to anyone in Omaha about moving here. It might be best not to take a chance. He'd stay here a few days and think on it.

CHAPTER 14

Roger woke in the morning with a vague feeling of unease. He had slept poorly, dreams of the past week waking him into a cold sweat. He had a headache, and had a sour taste in his mouth. He had spent a little too much time in the bar last night. He would check his mail today, check out the storage facility, and then look for someplace to stay, at least temporarily. Anything except an apartment. He hoped he would never live in another apartment.

Roger drug himself into the shower and let the water drain away the headache and the foggy feeling. He toweled off with the plush motel towels and walked naked back into his room. He was startled by his reflection in the mirror. A middle aged, slightly pudgy, gray haired man looked back at him. Was he Richard? Or Roger? He had to start thinking

Richard from now on.   He dressed and went to the motel restaurant for breakfast.

He checked USA Today for any new news on his situation.   Nothing there, he would have to find a Des Moines paper and see if they were still following the story.   He made a note to himself to do that today.

Roger finished his coffee and walked out to the Explorer in the parking lot. He got in and pulled out the Winslow map. He thought he might just drive around and see what was available. He picked up a local paper with the real estate listings and browsed through them. Nothing really caught his eye. He didn't want to be tied down in Winslow with a big mortgage, and he wasn't sure he wanted to rent anything either.   He wasn't sure what he wanted.   He decided just to drive around.

He drove first to the storage facility. Richard had rented a small unit and had several boxes stored in it. He opened the boxes and checked the contents.   They were filled with clothes, books, and memorabilia of Richard and his wife. No one would want or need them now. He sorted through the personal effects and saved a few of the pictures and papers. He might need to refer to them to perfect his transformation into his new identity. The rest of the papers he threw into the dumpster. Richards taste in books favored western novels, not Roger's idea of literature. He loaded the boxes of clothes and books into the Explorer and paid off the storage account. He drove around until he found a Salvation Army store and unloaded the boxes at their donation door.

That finished, Roger continued his drive around Winslow. It was a nice enough place, but nothing struck his eye. He found a news store, but they didn't carry any Iowa papers. He continued towards the edge of town, past liquor stores, bars and small shops. He was driving past car dealers when he saw a lot that was full of travel trailers and RV's. A sudden idea occurred to him. He could pull his home around with him. He wouldn't be tied to one area, and if he feared he was being discovered, he could move on.

Roger pulled into the lot. The front row was all RV's. He didn't think he would want that. He wanted to be able to park it and drive around without lugging his house with him. A travel trailer would fit the bill. He thought he could probably handle pulling one of those better too.

As he walked around the lot, he was amazed at the variety and types. Several were open, and he peered inside each, taking in the compactness of them. No space was wasted. There were cabinets everywhere. They had small kitchens, with stoves and sinks and even bathrooms. The orderly arrangements fitted with his style. This would be his home.

CHAPTER 15

Roger drove away from RV Village as the owner of a used 23-foot Road Ranger travel trailer. He was amazed at how inexpensive it was. He had paid cash for it, writing a check on Richards account. He had talked the salesman into taking a check and paid on the spot. It had dropped the balance of the checking account to a little over a hundred dollars, but he would transfer more in from the savings account when he found an ATM.

He was still carrying the gym bag full of money in the Explorer. He didn't want to leave it lying around the motel room. It was comforting to have all of that cash, but it was becoming a nuisance also. He knew he would need to drain the accounts into cash in case he had to abandon the Richard Whiteman identity. He was doing fine on Richards money so far. Maybe he could get a handy hiding place in his new RV. He could build up his cash reserves and live on the income from Richard.

He was to pick up the trailer the following day. The salesman said he would have it all set up and ready to go when he arrived. RV Village was arranging the insurance and registration for him. It would be registered in Nebraska until he established a permanent residence elsewhere. The Explorer already had a hitch, and the service department at RV Village had connected a wiring harness for him. He had larger mirrors installed for towing the trailer, and the salesman had walked him through the various hookups. The trailer was self-contained. It could operate for several days on it's own water supply and the batteries mounted behind the gas tanks on the front of the trailer. The propane gas operated the cooking stove, furnace and could run the refrigerator in case there wasn't any electricity available.

Roger decided he would park it here in Winslow for a while. He had to decide where he wanted to locate. He didn't feel comfortable here, this had been Richards idea, and he wanted to sever all ties to Richards old identity and establish his own.

He found a small trailer park not too far from the dealer. It had several vacancies with all of the hookups he would need for his new home. There was even a small Laundromat on the premises. He stopped in and rented a spot for a month. He hoped by then, he would have a destination in mind.

Roger drove back to the motel. His last night here, he would have a home again tomorrow. The idea appealed to him. He hadn't had a place of his own since he had lost his home to his creditors. Now he had a home, money in the bank, and freedom. Just like his mother always used to say, "All's well that ends well."

CHAPTER 16

Roger sat down in the dinette of his new home. He had picked up the trailer at 8 a.m., as soon as the lot opened this morning. He had his final instructions on operating the trailer and pulling one. He had never pulled anything behind a car before; it was a new experience. It had been much easier than he expected. He had pulled into his spot and unhooked like an old pro. Now he was all connected and had even made a cup of coffee in his kitchenette.

Stocking the trailer with food and supplies was his next step. There was a Super Wal-Mart just down the road; he imagined he could get everything he needed there. Roger was enjoying this new experience. He enjoyed the freedom, the choice to pick his own hours to sleep, when to eat and he could do whatever he wanted. Nobody to be responsible to or for. It was a great feeling.

Roger sorted through Richard's pictures and papers that he had saved from the storage room. There was a picture of Richard and a woman that Roger assumed was his wife. She had been a pretty woman, with long dark hair, dark eyes and a nice smile. Richard looked back at him with a smile of his own. He looked several years younger in the picture.

There were some older papers that documented the sale of a house in Omaha and another paper that was a copy of a security deposit at an apartment complex in Omaha. He studied the papers for a while and then stored them with his money in one of the many compartments in the trailer. The one paper he couldn't find was the title to the Explorer, although the registration was still in the glove box. That bothered him a little, but if he had to sell it, he could most likely get a duplicate title. The Explorer was fairly new and had only 25,000 miles on it. He planned on keeping it for as long as he could.

He checked the news daily. The local library had a computer and he found the Des Moines Register site and checked it daily. The story of the bank robbery and the deaths of Marian and Barbara had faded with the lack of new evidence. There was always new violence and crime to keep the papers busy. Roger really didn't think of himself as a criminal, he was more a victim of circumstance than anything else. His luck had been bad for years; it just took a violent turn of events to change it for him. This was the first time he had felt really happy in as long as he could remember. He felt more thankful than remorse about Richard. That had been a horrible experience. The ends justified the means for Roger. He had a whole new life now, thanks to Richard. That experience was over and done with. He had no great anticipation of what lay ahead of him, but more a sense of relief of what he had left behind.

CHAPTER 17

He enjoyed the trailer park. Most of the residents were snowbirds, coming to Arizona in the winter to escape the cold and snow of their northern homes. Roger avoided long conversations with any of them, usually just a "Good Morning", or "Hello". He had received a few invitations for dinner, which he had turned down with various excuses. Most of the exchanges were about their trailers or motor homes. Roger spent most of his time indoors, away from the heat of the day. Most of the others did too; it took some time to get used to the heat after leaving the winter of the north. Roger was comfortable with that also. He would either read or watch the small television in the trailer, mostly news programs, he didn't care for the inane sitcoms.

He bought a laptop computer at Wal Mart. The trailer court had wireless access, so he bought an HP with built in wireless capability. Now he could check the Des Moines Register online for any news from the privacy of his mobile home. He also signed up for online banking with Bank America. He could handle his finances online and transfer funds from one account to another as needed. He logged into Richards credit card account and got set up for online payment to his account. He had an account set up with MSN for his email address and bought a pay-as-you-go cell phone too. He could purchase more time on it as needed with his credit card. All the online sites wanted a daytime phone number to sign up, and now he had one. He got a model that he could connect to the laptop so that if he was in an area that didn't have wireless, he could use the cell phone as a modem. Now he was really mobile.

He would check his mail daily; nothing ever came except ads for "occupant". He had his mail transferred to a post office box. He notified the bank, and sent a change of address to his credit card account through the online service.   That   was   the   extent   of   his communications anymore.   His utilities were handled at the trailer park.   The first month had turned into a second month. He felt comfortable here, he had a routine established, and he had even gotten into the habit of having breakfast at the corner coffee shop.   After the first week, the waitress had asked his name and now greeted him with "Hello, Dick," when he walked in.   He had his usual booth and she always brought him a cup of coffee without being asked.   He was becoming a "regular".

CHAPTER 18

All of that changed and brought reality back with a jolt early on a Monday morning. Alice had brought his coffee and taken his order for breakfast when the door to the diner opened and a man in a police uniform walked in.

He stepped up to the counter and asked Alice, "I'm looking for Richard Whiteman, and they said at the trailer court that I could probably find him here. He around?"

Alice looked from the cop to Richard, a question in her eyes. He followed her look and spotted Roger in his booth. "That him?" he asked.

"Hey Dick, looks like the law has caught up with you." Alice joked.

Roger sat there, unable to move. He was glad he was sitting in the booth, had he been standing, he would have collapsed. He mustered up a sickly grin and raised a hand in greeting.

"I'm Richard Whiteman, how can I help you?"

"I'd like to ask you a few questions, you got a minute?" He asked as he slid into the booth opposite Roger. He motioned to Alice and pointed at Rogers cup. She nodded and brought a cup over.

"Use cream?"

"No thanks, black is fine." The cop answered and turned his gaze back to Roger.

"I'm lieutenant Walker, Mr. Whiteman, we've been asked to help in an investigation by the Iowa office of the F.B.I."

"Sure," said Roger, trying desperately to appear relaxed. "How can I possibly help?"

"There was a bank robbery and double homicide in Iowa a month or so ago, the trail ended in Omaha, just about the time you left. The Omaha and Iowa authorities are looking at any leads they might have from that time frame. Your name came up when they were checking the lists of people that had moved from Omaha that week. You left Omaha just about the time their suspect disappeared. They've checked flights, and bus departures; stuff like that, nothing has turned up. They figure he must have caught a ride with someone."

"Sorry I can't help, I drove down alone. I left the night I finished at Wal-Mart. I worked part time there in Omaha." Roger looked down at his hand holding the coffee cup. The knuckles were white. He forced himself to relax his grip. He fought against a tremble that was threatening his entire body.

Walker just stared at him for a second. Then he picked up his cup and took a deep swallow. "You mind if I have a look at your drivers license?"

Roger fumbled out his billfold and handed over the license. Walker picked it up and pulled a small notebook from his breast pocket. He made a few notes on the notebook and took a look at the picture of Richard on the front. "Looks like you've lost a little weight." He commented as he handed it back.

"Probably from eating my own cooking." Roger managed as he took the license. "My wife died since that picture was taken, a lot of things have changed since then."

Walker nodded and produced a slight smile, "Sorry to hear that. I just needed to check you out." He put the notebook back in his pocket and took another sip of his coffee.

"O.K., about what I figured. You know we have to check every lead." He slid out of the booth and reached for his wallet.

"I understand, and let me get that coffee for you lieutenant, you didn't get to finish it."

"Thanks Mr. Whiteman, and thanks for your time. Sorry to bother you." Walker smiled down at Roger, then turned and walked out the door.

"Hey desperado, what was that all about?" Alice was standing at the booth, coffeepot in hand. She refilled Rogers cup and picked up Walkers half full one.

"Nothing Alice, he was following up on a case up in Iowa and Nebraska, where I came from. Nothing to do with me."

"Sure made you nervous. I could see you squeezing that cup from where I stood. I thought it might shatter, you were squeezing it so hard." She grinned down at Roger, enjoying the moment.

Roger stuck the smile back on his face and took a sip from his cup, holding it with both hands and leaning into it. "Cops always make me nervous, don't they you?"

Alice grinned back at him, "Only when I'm guilty." She poured more coffee for him and went back behind the counter.

Roger sat in the booth. He wanted to get up and run. He could feel the sweat trickling down his sides. He kept his hands under the table, where the shaking couldn't be seen. He sat there, gradually gaining control again. He couldn't get upset like this. That would be taken as a sign that he was hiding something.

Alice brought his breakfast order over and set it in front of him. He had forgotten he had ordered before Walker had come in. Now he didn't have an appetite. He made himself eat it, just to keep Alice from wondering.

By the time he had finished choking down his breakfast, he had calmed down. He should have been expecting it. He just didn't think like a cop, that was all. It was only natural they would check something like that, wasn't it?

The next few days, Roger was seeing police cars everywhere he went. Had they always been around that much? Or were they watching him?

CHAPTER 19

Roger lasted three more weeks. He was getting over being paranoid about the cops, but he just felt he had to move on and find his own place. He really didn't care for Winslow all that much, it was o.k., but it was too hot, and there really wasn't all that much to keep him here. He had tried to make out with Alice, but it turned out she had a steady boyfriend, one about twice Roger's size, and he didn't have Alice's sense of humor.

With the travel trailer, he felt mobile. He thought he would like to travel a little, see some of the country. He never had traveled much as long as he had been married to Marian. He had always been busy at work, and the few vacations they took were usually one of the three-day cruises, or a short trip to Las Vegas. The cruises always bothered him because Marian wanted to shop at the expensive little shops, and he never was much for the cruise scene, mixing in the crowds, the dance parties. Roger was too much of a loner for all of that. He felt confined on the cruise boats. Las Vegas was better. He enjoyed the charged atmosphere, and seeing other people win the big jackpots. Roger didn't gamble much; he hated to lose.

He was ready. He had paid off his trailer spot, made arrangements to have his mail forwarded when he had a new address, and now he was hooked up and pulling out of the park. He drove out to the highway and turned west. He planned on driving until he found a spot that looked good, and then parking the trailer for a while. He felt he would know when he was in the right spot.

CHAPTER 20

Roger left Arizona and headed north to Las Vegas. He made it a three-day trip, stopping in a couple of campgrounds along the way. When he got to Las Vegas, he found a trailer park on Paradise Road, past the airport. They had several spots open and he picked one with a couple of palm trees for shade. He set up his trailer and connected his sewer pipe and water. He connected his power line to the thirty-amp service. There was no phone service available. Roger didn't mind; he wasn't expecting any calls anyway. He had his cell phone and there was a pay phone at the office he could use if necessary.

He drove to a Super Wal-Mart in Henderson, and picked up the groceries he needed. He took I-215 back to Paradise Road and when he got to the trailer, he unloaded his groceries and decided to take a run down the strip to see what was new since his last visit.

He took Paradise Road down to Tropicana Avenue, then down to Las Vegas Boulevard. He drove down the strip heading north. The imposing skyline of New York, New York, loomed on his left, the roller coaster making its loop as he passed. Traffic was fairly light for a Tuesday afternoon. It would pick up on the weekend, he knew.

It was amazing. Last time he had been here, the Aladdin was just being built. The newest hotel then was the Venetian. Las Vegas never stopped changing. New replaced old almost overnight. He could relate to that, just like his life. Roger liked the excitement that seemed to be in the air.

He continued down the strip, past the Aladdin, Bellagio's and the Mirage. As he neared the Stratosphere, he pulled into a Denny's restaurant. It was too early for dinner, but he was ready for a cup of coffee. He took a seat at the counter. No Alice here. The round-cheeked waitress had a nametag that read "Juanita".

"Cup of coffee, Sir?" She had a slight Spanish accent.

"Thanks, that would be fine." Roger replied. He looked around the dining area. There were slot machines lined up along one wall, several in use. The players had a cup of coffee in one hand and were playing the machines with the other. There was a constant cacophony of sound, as steady as background music.

There were Keno cards placed along the counter. Several monitors were mounted near the ceiling, displaying the results of the games. Roger pulled out one of the cards and a black crayon. He marked three spots for three plays at a dollar a play. He pulled three ones out of his billfold and held them with the card. A girl appeared at his elbow almost as soon as he held up the card. She took the money and the card and went to a corner table and came back with a printout with his numbers and the three games listed on it.

Roger wasn't a gambler, but playing the Keno would help him kill a little time while he had his coffee.

He hit one number the first game, none the second, but on the third, he hit all three numbers. He finished his coffee and put two dollars on the counter to pay for it. He took his Keno ticket to the table in the corner and handed it to the girl behind the machine. She smiled at him and put the ticket in the machine.

"Forty two dollars." She smiled. "Want to play again?"

"No thanks, I think I'll quit while I'm ahead" Roger put the money in his billfold and walked out of Denny's.

"Not bad, I just got forty dollars for drinking a cup of coffee." Roger mused to himself as he got back in the Explorer. He drove back down the strip and pulled into the parking in back of the Aladdin. He locked the Explorer and headed inside to the casino. Cool air and noise hit him simultaneously as he walked in the door. He wandered around the slot machines and then past the tables. Blackjack, roulette and crap tables ran along the walkway. Business was slow so far, it would pick up as the day went on.

Roger walked out to the shops. It was like walking into a mideastern bazaar. Stores lined both sides of a stone path. Jewelry stores, souvenir shops and clothing stores. Roger looked up at the ceiling and saw what appeared to be the sky above him. It was a huge painted mural that looked like the real sky. As he looked, it suddenly got darker and lightning flashed and was followed by a roll of thunder. He halfway expected raindrops to begin falling.

Roger smiled to himself at the wonder of it all. Soon, the "storm" ceased and the "sky" got lighter again. He walked into a small café that had all kinds of caviar for sale. You could purchase any amount from a small taste to a jar. He sampled a small taste of beluga caviar and washed it down with an ice-cold martini. His bill was twenty-two dollars. Too rich for his taste.

The shops seemed to go on forever. He picked up a brochure at one of the stands and learned that there was indeed over a mile of shops. He walked on completely around the line of shops and emerged once again into the casino.

He sat at one of the Keno areas and played several more games, no winners this time. Roger was getting bored. He wasn't about to start throwing money away on the casinos. Gambling just wasn't his bag. He walked back to the parking and got into the Explorer.

Roger felt secure in Las Vegas. Most of the crowds of people were from out of town. He fit right in with the throngs walking along the strip. He could stick around here for a while, and let his past fade away. No one would ever suspect him here. He could work on his Richard Whiteman identity. Time was on his side now.

CHAPTER 21

He drove back to the trailer and parked in the shade. The sun was blazing in the sky above. It was warm in the trailer. He turned on the air conditioning and took one of his folding chairs back outside. He set up the chair and went back in and got a coke out of the refrigerator.

Roger leaned back in the chair and relaxed. It was warm in the shade and he was comfortable, with his feet stretched out in front of him.

He thought about all of the transients here in Las Vegas. This would probably be a good spot to pick up a fall back identity. Like it or not, he knew that eventually, the Richard Whiteman I.D. would collapse. He needed at least one other identity for emergency. He had no idea what to do for the long term.

He purchased a small suitcase and put in some spare clothes and $5,000 in cash from his reserves. He had rented a small storage shed near the airport, using his Richard Whiteman drivers' license and paying six months rent. He left the suitcase inside. The gate to the facility was opened with a four-digit code. His unit was locked with a combination padlock, so there was no key to keep track of. At least now, he had a fallback hideaway for emergencies.

CHAPTER 22

He had dozed off and was wakened by the sound of tires rolling on the gravel drive by his trailer. He opened his eyes and saw a black and white police cruiser slowly driving by. The officer behind the wheel was looking at him through mirrored sunglasses, a serious expression on his face. The cruiser stopped and the driver's window rolled down.

"You O.K. mister?" The cop asked.

"Hi, yeah, I'm fine, just dozed off." Roger stammered.

"Sorry to bother you, but you looked like you might have passed out." The officer grinned back at him, letting his elbow hang out the window. "You sure didn't look comfortable with your head hanging back like that."

Roger grinned back and rubbed the back of his neck. "Thanks, I'm fine."

The cop gave a two fingered salute and rolled on past. Roger watched him as he drove down the trailer park lane. He was checking each trailer as he drove past. Probably just routine. He watched until the car rolled out onto Paradise and headed back towards the city. Roger was pleased with his lack of nervousness.

"They keep a good watch on us." The voice startled Roger and he whirled around to see where it came from.

A man several years his junior was standing by the motor home next to Rogers trailer. He was wearing an open shirt and shorts and had sandals on with no socks. He scratched a slightly round belly with his left hand and held out his right.

"Hi neighbor, my names Ron, Ron Mayer."

"Richard, er, Dick, Whiteman. Nice to meet you." Roger shook hands as he rose from his chair.

"LVPD makes a pass through here at least once a day. Pretty sharp outfit. Makes you feel secure, knowing they're looking out for you."

"Yeah, that helps. You been here long?" Roger moved back into the shade to stand next to Mayer.

"Two weeks. Wife and I are on an extended vacation. I took a thirty-day leave of absence. I'm getting over an operation and need some time to heal up. I plan on staying another week, then heading back to Seattle."

"Oh? Nothing serious, I hope."

"Kidney transplant. Operation was a breeze, but all the pills and stuff after are knocking me out."

"Sorry to hear that. What do you do in Seattle?"

"Website administrator." Ron grinned, "I know, it's usually the kids that do that, but I've been in computers ever since I got out of high school. I'm doing what I like. I can do a lot of work from here on my laptop, but I get a lot of my material as hard copy and I'll need to get back eventually. I've got a partner covering for me back home. How about you?"

"Semi-retired." Said Roger, "My wife died of cancer about a year ago. I quit work to take care of her. I was an over the road driver." The story came easy to him now. It was second nature to him. Conversations like this helped him fine-tune his background.

"Too bad, that cancer is terrible stuff. My wife's in town shopping. She generally takes off while I take a nap in the afternoon. Works for both of us." Mayer looked over Rogers trailer. "How do you like the Road Ranger?"

"Great, it's plenty big for me, and it's easy to pull and park."

"We like the motor home, we pull our little Geo Metro behind it. I've got a place in Seattle I store it when we're not on the road. Like to take a look inside?"

Roger had found out that this was a standard ritual among RV'ers. You had to check out each other's lodging.

"Sure," said Roger, and they headed into Mayer's motor home. A blast of cool air greeted them as he opened the door. The interior was very plush. It had a tip out in the living room that added a lot of space. A small kitchenette was between the living room and a large bedroom at the rear. A small bathroom was next to the bedroom. Again, Roger was amazed at the utilization of every square inch of space. Storage everywhere; and all the comforts of home.

"Really nice." Roger said, "Makes my trailer look tiny by comparison."

"Yeah, we like it. Sure beats staying in motels."

They exchanged small talk for a while and Roger gave Mayer a tour of his trailer. Mayer was impressed at how neat Roger kept it. Roger promised to stop by later to meet his wife, Kay. Ron headed back to his motor home for his nap, and Roger moved back inside his trailer.

He had enjoyed his conversation with Mayer. He kept in role and was Dick Whiteman. He felt he actually was Dick Whiteman. He knew his role better than his own miserable life. He had considered Mayer as another identity, but the physical resemblance was too different. Strange at how he looked at people anymore.

CHAPTER 23

Roger met Kay Mayer later that day. She was a pleasant, slightly overweight lady with premature gray hair and a charming smile and ready laugh. She fussed over Ron continually, obviously worried about his condition. They had hamburgers fixed on the grill and Roger furnished a bottle of wine that he and Kay shared, Ron sticking to water.

They talked until the sun started to set; then Roger went back to his trailer to read until his bedtime. He envied the Mayer's their relationship. He and Marian had never been that close. He was feeling comfortable here. Outside of the minor incident with the patrolman that afternoon, everything was going nicely.

He thought that maybe tomorrow, he would look at some of the street people.

Possibly there was another identity waiting to be harvested. Somehow, the idea was not totally repugnant to Roger

CHAPTER 24

The Mayers had left for Seattle. The spot next to Roger was still vacant. It was the second week in June; the spaces would all be filled soon with vacationers. So far, he was paying by the week. He liked this location, it was far enough away from town to avoid the heavier traffic, but still close enough if he wanted to go in and wander the casinos. He liked to catch a show now and then too. Roger enjoyed driving Las Vegas Boulevard, watching the crowds flow up and down the sidewalks, going in and out of the casinos and tourist traps.

The weather was getting hot. He kept the little rooftop air conditioner running most of the time. The trailer didn't take long to cool off, and the palm trees provided enough shade to block a lot of the sun's rays. He had been smart to pick a spot with trees. There was a playground in the park, but it was mostly deserted during the heat of the day. Children came to it in the evening, after the sun went down. It was well lit and surrounded with a chain link fence. The sound of the kids playing was comforting, their laughter and screams giving the park a lived in feel.

Roger had a routine going again. He would stop at the diner near the airport for breakfast, watching the airplanes landing at McCarran airport. After breakfast, he returned to the trailer and did his morning cleaning and any laundry that needed done. He usually changed the bed and did laundry on Wednesday mornings, when the Laundromat was nearly empty. Grocery shopping was on Thursday. Most weekends, he would spend either on the strip, or in the old part of Las Vegas along Fremont Street, watching the crowds. The light show at night was always entertaining. He played a little Keno, and a slot machine once in awhile. He tried blackjack a couple of times, but didn't enjoy playing in the larger casinos, where the minimum bet was three dollars. He had found a little casino on one of the side streets that had one-dollar minimum bets and played there occasionally.

He enjoyed the buffet dinners. A lot of food for the price. Although Roger wasn't a big eater, he did like bargains. The buffet at the Riviera was one of his favorites, but the lines were long. Even though the casinos were crowded on weekends, that was when Roger would eat out. He enjoyed watching the crowds. None of them suspected that he was a wanted criminal. He got a charge out of that. If they only knew.

He kept his eye out for single males that matched his physical characteristics. He had found few that matched his criteria. He realized now how lucky he had been to run into Richard when he did. It was as if fate had decided his path for him and provided what he needed, when he needed it. He accepted that and felt as though fate was finally looking out for him, trying to make up for all those years of disappointment. If he didn't find someone soon, he would have to move on. He didn't feel comfortable staying in one spot so long.

CHAPTER 25

Roger was in a hurry. It was the Thursday after the Fourth of July weekend. Traffic was heavy and it was hot. He was on his way back to the trailer after grocery shopping. He had been stuck behind an eighteen-wheeler that had engine trouble. Traffic was backed up and moving slowly. Roger cut around a tourist in a mini-van and cut through a corner after the light had changed. He had just slowed down when he saw the lights flashing in his mirrors.

He pulled over to the side of the road and waited as the black and white LVPD cruiser stopped behind him, lights still flashing. A Las Vegas police officer got out of the car and approached him on the driver's side, one hand resting on the holstered pistol at his side. He was dressed in the summer khaki uniform and wore mirrored sunglasses.

Roger rolled down his window. He had his license and registration in his hand as the officer stopped.

"You ran the stop sign back at the corner. I was right behind you." The officer said as he took the license and registration. "I'm afraid I'm going to have to give you a ticket."

"I'm sorry," Roger said, "I was in a hurry to get home, my ice cream is melting. I've been stuck in a traffic jam."

"Well, you would have gotten there sooner by obeying the law." The cop was writing the ticket. "You from Nebraska?"

"Yes, I'm traveling now. I'm staying at the RV park out by the airport."

He handed Roger the ticket and looked again at the license and registration. "You better be getting this renewed before long, you have a birthday this month, you know."

"Yes, yes, I intend to." Roger took the license and stuck it back in his billfold.

"You can either send in the payment on the ticket, pay it at the office, or appear in court at the date specified on the ticket. Watch your driving. I ran your license and you came back clean. You have a good driving record, don't mess it up."

"Thanks officer, I'm sorry about the light. Won't happen again." Roger took the ticket and put his registration back in the glove box. The cop was still standing by the window, looking at Roger. Roger was getting nervous, anxious to be out of there.

Finally the cop stepped back, "Have a nice day." He said, and turned back to his patrol car. The lights quit flashing and he pulled around Roger and drove on down the street.

Roger sat there for a few minutes. What a stupid stunt. He sure didn't need to attract attention from the police. He put the car in gear and pulled cautiously back into traffic. He drove under the speed limit all the way back to the trailer, stopping and checking at each intersection.

By the time he arrived at the trailer, his ice cream was a mess. He threw it in the garbage and put away the rest of the groceries. Then he sat at the dinette, calming himself down. He wrote out a check for the ticket and put postage on it. He sure didn't want to be late getting it paid. He would drop it in the mailbox at the office his next trip out. He would have to check on renewing his license too. He couldn't afford to have that expire on him. He would send a letter to the department of motor vehicles in Nebraska.

He had gotten complacent and over confidant again. He had to remember to be always aware of what could happen if the police ran a fingerprint check on him. That would be sure to finish him. Richard had served in the military, so his prints would be on file. Roger had his prints taken back on his old job and then again, when he started at the bank. He must be careful.

CHAPTER 26

Roger started noticing more police cars. It seemed that everywhere he went he saw one. The Las Vegas Police had both the cars and SUV's, the same black and white paint jobs with the POLICE decals on the side. When he was downtown, he saw the bicycle patrols, the officers with the yellow jerseys. If it wasn't the Las Vegas police, it was the Clark County Sheriffs cars. Every time he saw one, he reacted by slowing down and driving cautiously until they were out of sight.

He had been cruising the strip on a Saturday night when he was startled by flashing lights in his mirrors again. He pulled over to the side. He knew this was going to be it. He was reaching for his billfold, when the cruiser pulled around him and headed after a car ahead of him. He quickly pulled back into traffic and took a right at the next corner. He got on Paradise

Road and drove back to the trailer. His hands were shaking as he unlocked the door.

Maybe it was time to move on. If he found a smaller community, he might be able to relax more. He had been jumpy ever since he had gotten that ticket for running the light. His rent for his spot was due Monday. He decided to let it go and get back on the road. As soon as he made that decision, he began to feel comfortable again. That must be the right way to go.

The next morning, he got the trailer ready to travel. He would stop by the office in the morning and let them know he was moving on. By Sunday evening he was all ready to go. A new identity would have to wait. There would be other opportunities.

CHAPTER 27

Roger had left early that morning after checking out at the office. He had taken I-15 up to Highway 95 and was now heading north on 95. He stopped at Tonopah Monday afternoon and decided to stay there overnight. He would decide in the morning, which way to go.

Tuesday morning, Roger had decided to try Winnemucca. Reno would be too much like Las Vegas. Winnemucca was much smaller. Besides, he liked the name of the town. He drove through the Big Smokey Valley, then turned onto U.S. 50, sometimes known as "Loneliest Road", as far as highway 305. He headed north on 305 to Battle Mountain. There was a sign welcoming everyone to Battle Mountain, "The armpit of the U.S. Make us your 'pit' stop". He caught I-80, and then took the interstate into Winnemucca. There was an RV park just off the interstate on the north side

119

of Winnemucca. He parked the trailer there and drove in to get a look at downtown. He could tell the elevation here was higher than Las Vegas. The air felt cooler and cleaner. Winnemucca didn't have a whole lot. There were a few casinos and several motels with casinos in the lobbies. Roger had a quick dinner at a café and headed back to the trailer.

He didn't think he could stay here. It felt crowded, with the interstate running by it. There wasn't much to do, and he hadn't seen a really nice RV park that he would care to stay in for a long period of time. He decided to stay for a couple of days, and then figure out which way to head. At least he hadn't seen a single cop all day.

CHAPTER 28

Roger had his atlas on the dinette, a cup of coffee setting beside it. It was a bright, clear day in this high desert country. He could hear the birds chirping outside and the noise of the traffic on the interstate came to him faintly. He looked at his choices. More Nevada, Idaho, Oregon and California. He had been in Utah, and knew it was too barren for him. He was torn between Oregon and California.

He got a quarter out of his pocket and flipped it. "Heads, California, Tails, Oregon." The coin bounced on the tabletop and rolled to a stop. Tails were up. "Oregon, here I come."

CHAPTER 29

He took highway 95 north, and then turned west on 140. He heeded the signs warning him to fill up before starting highway 140. It was a deserted two-lane road with very little traffic and a stark beauty to it. He saw signs for wild donkey crossings, and then actually saw a herd of them. Towns were few and far between. Denio could barely be called a town. He gassed up at Denio Junction and drove through switchbacks and narrow roads until he reached Oregon. He drove through a pass with a spectacular view and a steep mountain road to the valley below. He stopped for breakfast at Lakeview, Oregon.

He passed around Klamath Falls and kept heading west. Some of the mountain roads were a little exciting, especially when the logging trucks came roaring down the road. He finally came to highway 62 in Oregon. There were signs for Crater Lake. Something seemed to beckon to him, so he headed north. He stopped for gas in a small town named Shady Glen on the Rogue River. What a beautiful spot. It was a small town, less than 3,000 population. It was located in the Rogue River valley and stretched out along the river for about five miles. It was surrounded by pine-covered hills.

He decided to pull into one of the many RV parks. He found a small park on the north side of town that sat right next to the river. This should be a good place to park. He checked in at the office, unhooked the trailer and went into town for groceries.

Roger decided to stay for a while. He hadn't picked up any mail since he left Las Vegas, not that there would be much, just a bank and credit card statements. He had the bank making automatic payments to the credit card. He stopped in the post office and made arrangements to have his mail forwarded from

Winslow. On impulse, he rented a post office box. He sent a change of address back to Winslow. He would use Shady Glen for a base for now.

He got back into a routine. His coffee spot now was a restaurant named "Twin Pines". "Donna" had taken the place of "Alice" in Winslow. He stopped in Twin Pines about every morning to have breakfast and read the news. He hadn't seen anything about the robbery and deaths for months. It had to be a cold case by now; it had been almost five months. He never had seen anything about Richard's body turning up.

Roger took up fishing. He had rented some equipment at first, not knowing if he'd like it or not. He had never tried fishing before. It turned out that he really enjoyed it. It was relaxing and helped pass the time. He had bought his own equipment after the first try. He never kept any of the fish; he used the "catch and release" method of fishing. He knew nothing about cleaning fish and had no desire to learn. They fixed excellent fish dinners at Twin Pines, his cooking was minimal.

One warm summer day, he was fishing near the trailer park. He was working his way upstream in his new waders, casting to likely spots as he went. He had a few hits, but hadn't hooked anything yet.

"Good morning,"

Roger nearly fell into the water at the sound. He turned and saw another fisherman between him and the bank. The man was half hidden in the shadows. He was tall and lanky. His eyes were hidden behind aviator dark glasses.

"Sorry, I didn't see you there." Roger stammered.

"That's o.k., I was just getting ready to leave for work anyway." Said the stranger. "Didn't mean to startle you like that."

"Name's Gary, Gary Frost." He held out his hand to Roger.

"Richard, or Dick, Dick Whiteman." Roger shook hands with Gary. "Nice to meet you."

"Are you new around here?" Gary asked, "I haven't seen you around."

"I'm sort of a temporary resident, I have a travel trailer at the Shady Trails Park.

"We get lots of temporaries here, especially during the fishing season." Gary said, wading up to the bank. "I guess you could say I'm a permanent resident, I've lived here for five years now."

Roger waded up the bank with Gary. He was ready to head back for the day. It was time for breakfast at Twin Pines. They walked together towards the parking lot by the river. Roger loaded his fishing tackle into the back of the Explorer, and Gary set his in the back of an old pickup truck.

"Probably see you around, in a town this small, it's hard not to see each other." Gary smiled at Roger. "Nice meeting you, Dick. Have a good one." Gary swung open the drivers door and got into his pickup.

"Same here, Gary. See you." Roger waved as he got in his Explorer. He waited for Gary to pull out, and then followed him into town. Gary pulled off on a side street, and waved out the window as he turned. Roger waved back and continued on to Twin Pines for breakfast.

Roger sat in his usual booth and opened the paper. Donna headed towards him, coffee pot in hand.

CHAPTER 30

"What'll it be this morning Dick?   The eggs or the pancakes." Donna poured his coffee and sat the pot on the table and pulled out her pad.

"Think I'll do the pancakes this morning Donna. I had a hard morning fishing already." Roger smiled up at her.

"Sounds like a tough life."   Donna smiled back. "Don't see how you handle it."

"Taint easy." Roger was enjoying his conversation; Donna was pretty and witty. "Met another fishing slave this morning.   Name's Gary Frost, you know him?"

Donna laughed, "Sure, everybody in town knows Gary. He's our local Gestapo."

CHAPTER 31

The smile froze on Rogers face. "He's a cop?"

"Sure is. One of our six, and the top dog. He's our chief." Donna was writing down Rogers order as she spoke. She didn't see the reaction on Rogers face.

Roger got himself back under control. It was no big deal; he was bound to meet another cop sometime. This local yokel would be no threat to him.

Donna was still talking, "Yep, Gary's quite a catch for a town this size, he had ten years with L.A.P.D., he was a big shot investigator there. He said he was burned out with all the monsters in Los Angeles, wanted something a little more laid back. L.A.'s loss was our gain." Donna headed back to the kitchen with Roger's order.

Roger pondered this latest information. Big investigator. Still, he was two thousand miles and months away from his problem. He had been through several tests of his credibility, and passed them all. Time to get over it. He'd be careful of course, no sense being careless now.

Roger finished breakfast, and headed back to his trailer. He made up his bed and got his laundry ready to take to the Laundromat. They didn't have one in this park, but he used the one in town. He had moved his money from the gym bag into a hard side briefcase that he kept locked and hidden in the trailer. He had been moving small amounts from his bank accounts over the last several months, building up his emergency fund. He kept changing to larger denomination bills as he could without attracting attention, and still, the case was getting full. He might need another case if this kept up. He had sent another check to the storage facility in Las Vegas. His hideaway was good for another year.

He was getting Richards retirement checks direct deposited each month. With the retirement and Richard's social security, he was getting nearly fifteen hundred a month. Plenty enough to live on. Roger knew he'd have to file income tax this year if he stayed with the Richard Whiteman identity. He was watching his finances carefully. He didn't want to attract attention from the IRS. He was glad he was a CPA; he wouldn't make the mistakes that others might.

He had contacted the Nebraska Department of Motor Vehicles and gotten a digital photograph forwarded to them. The state of Nebraska would issue a drivers license through the mail to out of state addresses. Luckily, again. Richard had changed his commercial license to a regular operators license. Otherwise, Roger would not have been able to renew by mail. He had sent a copy of Richards license along with the fee and now had a current Nebraska drivers' license.

Roger drove into town and put his clothes in the washer. They'd be o.k. while he walked across the street to the grocery store and picked up a few things. That was one of the nice things about this small town, nobody locked their doors, and nobody worried about thieves.

Roger picked up a frozen pizza for his dinner, some of that great Oregon wine, and a few other groceries. He paid and carried his small sack over and put it in the rear of the Explorer. The wash cycle was over, so Roger put his clothes in the dryer. Fifteen minutes and he'd be heading back to his trailer. Home.

He liked his simple life here. The trailer was cozy, plenty big enough for him. His monthly rent for his spot was just two hundred dollars. He had cable TV, a phone and water and sewer hookups. His grocery bill was never over two hundred a month, and that was about the extent of his expenses. He had his morning routine at Twin Pines, his fishing and he got enough exercise walking around town and fishing. His health was good; life was good.

Roger never dwelled on the past. What was done was done. He didn't miss Marian; they hadn't been getting along well for years. She would have felt the same if she were in his shoes. Barbara? Ha! He sure didn't miss that bitch. Maybe he had her to thank though. If she hadn't slipped and cracked her head, he wouldn't be here, living this good life now. He smiled at the thought. Too bad about Richard, though, he had kind of liked Richard. He wasn't all gone if you looked at it right, they shared the same identity now. Richard would have liked it here too.

CHAPTER 32

Gary Frost sat at his desk in front of his computer. He had picked up a strange vibe from Dick Whiteman. Nothing particular, just a feeling. He had automatically memorized his license number and was now running the plate and Richards name through NCIC. He felt a little guilty, but it was an old habit he had picked up at LAPD. He ran names all of the time, usually nothing came up, but once in a great while, he got a hit. Back child support, old traffic warrants, nothing spectacular.

Nothing on Richard Whiteman, nothing criminal, anyway. He felt a slight sense of relief. He had enjoyed their conversation. He could relate to Richards solitary life. It was too similar to his own. No ties, no family, nobody to answer to, except for the job. Gary was tied to the job and it was a part of him. Probably not the best part either; it had taken over his life.

Whatever, he thought, *didn't have that much of a life anyway*. Since his divorce, Gary had devoted about all of his time to the job. Up here in Shady Glen, it wasn't all that demanding. That had suited him fine too, until the letter from L.A.

He did find some interesting things about Richard. He had been a marine in Korea, awarded a bronze star. He had worked until two years ago with an over-the-road trucking company based in Omaha. The company had been sold to a larger firm recently. His wife had died of cancer about two months after he had retired and then he had worked at Wal-Mart part time for a while. No kids, no immediate family.

Gary got some of this info from NCIC, most from the Omaha Herald. Usually, the newspapers had more information about a person than the government did. Gary had found that out early in his law-enforcement career. If you wanted to find out about someone, dig into the newspaper archives.

135

He had enough to know he didn't want to pry anymore into Richards past. He had fulfilled his obligation as the chief of police, now he'd let it rest. Richard wasn't a wanted criminal, that's all he cared about.

CHAPTER 33

Two weeks later, Roger was at the Twin Pines restaurant. It was fairly crowded this morning. He had his booth and was reading the paper. He had finished his breakfast and was lingering over his coffee, catching up on the news.

"Hi, mind if I join you?" It was Gary Frost, the chief of police.

"Hi, have a seat." Roger motioned across the table. He was in control this time.

"It's kind of crowded in here this morning, must be a bunch of new tourists in town. Hope they don't make any work for me." Gary smiled at the last remark. He was in uniform this morning, all dark blue with a shining badge. He put his cap on the table and smiled up at Donna, who had appeared at the table. "Hi, Donna, how about a cup of that stuff you call coffee."

Donna had brought a cup with her and sat it down in front of him. "Had you figured out already. You here to arrest Dick?"

Gary grinned over at Roger then back to Donna, "Nope, I don't need any extra work. If I needed to arrest anybody, it would probably be you, for poisoning your customers."

Donna pulled out her pad, "Ha, what can I poison you with this morning?"

"How about some ham and eggs. Don't suppose you can ruin that."

Donna scribbled on her pad, "I'll try." She grinned at the two of them and headed for the kitchen.

"What a trip, she starts my day off right." Gary smiled over at Roger, taking a sip of the hot coffee. "This is pretty good stuff, but don't ever tell Donna I said so."

Roger smiled back. "Caught any big salmon or steelhead lately?"

"Actually, I did. Big salmon." He held his hands apart about two feet, "I had it steaked out. Usually, I just catch and release, but I could imagine how great it would be with some wild rice and salad."

"Doesn't sound bad." Roger said, surprised that he actually meant it.

"I'll let you know when I'm fixing it. Maybe you could come over. There's plenty for two."

"I might just do that, I could even bring the wine." Roger was beginning to think it sounded like a good idea.

"I'll be in touch, probably this week-end." Gary sat back as Donna placed his ham and eggs in front of him.

"Over easy, just like you like them, with just a sprinkling of cyanide." Donna quipped.

"Mmmm! Sounds great." Gary picked up his fork and a piece of toast and started on his breakfast.

They exchanged small talk and left together, waving good-byes to Donna.

Gary was parked next to Roger in the lot. "Don't forget about salmon steaks, I'll be giving you a holler."

Roger waved and opened the door to the Explorer. "You got a deal." He got in and started up. He fastened his seat belt and followed Gary out of the lot. Turning left to go to his trailer, as Gary turned right.

Why not? he thought, *I might find out more about him, and he would be less likely to snoop into my life.*

The more he thought about it, the better it sounded to him. By the time he arrived at the trailer, he had decided to take Gary up on his offer, if he called.

They passed each other several times that week. They would wave and smile and continue on. Roger was beginning to believe that Gary had forgot about the invite. That would be o.k. too. Then, Friday, Gary was at Twin Pines when Roger came in for breakfast.

"Hey Dick, how's it going?" Gary was at the register, paying his bill.

"Just great Gary, how about you?"

"Fine, say, how about that salmon dinner tomorrow night? I was going to call you today."

"Sure, what kind of wine you like with that?"

"You pick one out, I'm not particular, as long as it's Oregon wine."

"Is there any other?" Roger grinned back, playing along with the local concept of wines. He was beginning to feel like a native.

141

"You got it.   Great. Dick, see you tomorrow night, come over any time, probably eat about six, you got my address?"

"No, I don't. It might help."

"It's 222 Ridge Road, know where that's at?" Gary picked up his change, looking back up at Roger.

"Yes, matter of fact I do. Nice area of town, pretty view."

"I like it.   See you tomorrow."   Gary headed out to the lot as Roger turned back and headed for his booth.

Later that morning, Roger stopped at the grocery store and picked up a bottle of Oregon Pinot Noir. That was supposed to go good with salmon. He thought over what he would do and say at Gary's.   He felt comfortable with his adopted identity. If he could get through the dinner with Gary, it would boost his confidence even more.

142

CHAPTER 34

It was a beautiful day. Roger had looked forward to the dinner. He thought he could like Gary. It would be a plus to have him as a friend.

He was a little surprised at Gary's house. It was larger than he thought it would be. The yard was nicely landscaped and there was a large pine tree at the corner of the lot that provided shade from the afternoon sun. There was a two-car garage at the end of the drive. Gary's pickup was parked on one side of the drive, and his patrol car on the other. Roger parked behind the pickup. He took his bottle of wine and walked to the door. Gary opened the door as he stepped on the small front deck.

"Hi Dick, see you brought a bottle of wine, hope it's from Oregon." Gary grinned at him as they shook hands.

143

"You bet, I got that Pinot Noir from Bridgeview winery, that o.k. with you? I like it better than Chardonnay with salmon."

"Sounds great! I hope my salmon is good enough for it. It should, it's Oregon salmon."

Gary led the way into a neat, well-furnished living room. "Have a seat, I'll open this wine."

Roger walked around the room, taking in the furnishings and artwork hanging on the walls. Definitely a mans house, no feminine touches here. There was a picture of a woman and a small girl on the mantle over the fireplace. Roger moved over for a closer look.

"That's my ex and my daughter. They live in L.A." Gary was back, two wine glasses in his hands. "It's an old picture, my daughter is 17 now."

"Nice looking family. You keep in touch?"

"Yes, we do. Mostly email now, couple of times a week and daily with my daughter. My wife couldn't handle my job in L.A. I was too stubborn to quit. By the time I came to my senses, she had left and re-married. He's a decent guy; he's been a real good father for my daughter, probably a better one than I would have been. She was only two when we separated. Linda, that's my daughter, spends a couple of weeks in the summer with me here, she likes this area."

"That's great that your daughter comes to see you. Too bad about your marriage though, so you never remarried?"

"Nope, I'm still a cop, it wouldn't be any different, the job still comes first, even here in Shady Glen."

"I can relate. I miss my wife, but I don't want to get married again. I enjoy my independence too much." Roger took the proffered glass of wine and took a sip. "Man, that's good wine." He wanted to change the subject.

"Yeah, I understand how you feel, it's kind of nice, having the freedom. You did good with the wine, that just so happens to be one of my favorites."

Gary took a seat in one of the easy chairs, and Roger sat down opposite him. They both sat quietly, enjoying the wine.

"I've got the grill fired up, won't take it long to heat up."

"That's fine, I can wait. Anything you need me to do?"

"Nope, the rice is boiling right now, I'll slap the salmon steaks on in a minute and everything should be done about the same time. I've got a salad on the table."

146

Gary took another sip of wine, then stood. "Let's go out in the kitchen where we can talk while I finish up." He headed back that way and Roger got up and followed him.

"Where did you work before Dick, I gather you're retired now?"

"I retired about two years ago. Used to be a trucker."

"Oh, what company?"

"It was a small local company. Named Turner and Son. We hauled produce. They just sold out recently. I worked there until my wife got cancer, then I retired to take care of her. She only lasted a month, went real quick. I didn't have anything to keep me in Omaha, so I headed out. I bought the trailer on impulse and I've been traveling since." It was the story Roger had developed from Richard's history.

Gary nodded, "What kind of rig did you drive?"

Roger was taken back, he hadn't thought about anybody asking that. "Uh, we had several different trucks."

"Eighteen wheelers?"

"Yeah, we pulled trailers with them." Roger was getting nervous with this line of questions, why hadn't he thought about this? He knew nothing about the big trucks.

"Ha," Gary laughed, "You don't sound anything like the truckers I know. They talk for hours about their rigs and what they'd carry. You sure you were a driver?"

Roger was getting nervous again. "Well, I really hadn't driven that much the last few years, I was always good with numbers, so they had me working on the books more. You know, with Mary, my wife, being ill and all."

Gary was looking at him funny. He was about to say something when a timer dinged on the counter. Gary looked at it, then got up and headed for the back deck. "Time to put the salmon on. I want it to get done the same time as the rice."

Roger let out a breath. Whew! He had to keep away from that line of conversation. He wanted to learn more about Gary, not the other way around. He had goofed, saying he had quit driving when his wife got sick, he had just said he had retired when she got cancer.

He followed Gary out on the deck. Gary was putting the salmon steaks on the grill. "I use mesquite chips when I'm grilling salmon. It adds something to the flavor."

Roger could smell the mesquite; the aroma was terrific. "Sure smells like it could. Man, that smells good."

"Yeah, my Mary had been sickly for several years before she got cancer. I always felt guilty for being gone so much. It still bothers me to talk about it."

149

Gary looked up from his grilling, "Sorry, I didn't mean to pry, I just thought all you truckers talked about your rigs all of the time."

"Yeah, well, I guess I did before the guilt trip, I've kind of got away from it. Don't talk about that time much anymore."

"Here, Dick, would you watch these steaks for a minute, I'm going in to get the rice ready." Gary handed Roger the fork and went back into the kitchen.

Roger felt he had covered that pretty well. Probably got Gary steered away from talking about trucking too.

They had a really good meal, finishing the bottle of wine, and opening another. The subject of trucking didn't come up again. They talked world news and discovered they shared political views and ideas about solutions to the world's problems. Gary had told some war stories about his time with the LAPD and he told Roger his thoughts about retuning to the city. They cleared the table together and Gary put the dishes in the dishwasher. He had bought some brownies and they were having them and coffee when Roger decided it was time to leave.

"Thanks for the great chow and conversation Gary, I probably better get going, about my bedtime" he said, "hope I can return the favor sometime."

"My pleasure" Gary got up with Roger and walked him to the door. "We'll have to get together again. I think we've about got the world figured out."

Roger laughed a real laugh, first one in a long time. "Too bad we aren't the world leaders."

He waved a good night and walked out to the Explorer. Gary waved and went back inside. Roger drove back to the trailer, rehashing the night. Other than the gaff about trucking, he thought it had gone pretty well. He had a much better insight to Gary's personality.

151

He was impressed with the obvious professionalism with which Gary handled his job. Some of his stories of his time in L.A. revealed a dedicated policeman, totally involved with his career. He realized he would have to be careful around Gary, very careful.

CHAPTER 35

Roger became known around Shady Glen. He was friendly enough, made some acquaintances, and became sort of a fishing buddy with Gary. They went fishing a couple of Sundays a month. They would rent a boat and spend the day on the water, packing a lunch and making a day of it. They would have dinner together one Saturday a month, taking turns being the host.

He went out with Donna occasionally. They would catch a movie and dinner in Medford. After the third time out together, she stayed over that night. They had a good relationship, neither wanting to move in with the other, they both treasured their independence. She had talked Roger into joining the community builders, a volunteer group that had improvement projects around town. They would have fundraisers and bake sales and the like. Roger was soon elected treasurer for the group and kept the books for them.

For the most part, he kept to himself. He enjoyed his trailer and walks along the river. He felt more secure each passing day. The past was fading away. Donna still came over occasionally. He went fishing with Gary. He was beginning to feel like he was Dick Whiteman.

That fall, he purchased a small piece of land further up the river. The previous owner had set it up for a trailer. He had a small plot for a garden and a semi-private drive. With Gary's help, he set up a small shed for gardening tools and fishing equipment. Next summer, he would plant a small vegetable garden. His hidden money kept growing. He had nearly $200,000 stashed away. It was another source of comfort knowing it was available if he needed it.

CHAPTER 36

It was a warm Friday morning. Roger had been thinking of this trip for some time. Ever since he had dinner with Gary, he had thought this might be a good idea.

He packed his small suitcase with a few clothes, added fifteen thousand from his cash supply and stuck in his shaving kit. As an afterthought, he put a hanger with sport coat and slacks on the clothes hook over the back door of the Explorer.

He locked the trailer and headed towards I-5. He rolled down the driver's side window and hung his arm on the door. He had "Mozart's Greatest Music" playing on the CD player. "Eine Kleine Nachtmusik" was filling the Explorer with sound. Roger had the stereo cranked up, enjoying the melody.

He pulled into San Francisco at six o'clock that evening. He took Embarcadero into the waterfront area and pulled into the Holiday Inn at Fisherman's Wharf. He got a suite on the third floor with a view of the Marina. Tonight, he'd just relax and enjoy the area. Tomorrow would be the start of phase one of his plan.

CHAPTER 37

Roger showered and shaved and dressed in slacks and shirt, then donned his sport jacket to ward off the perpetual chill of the bay area. He checked himself in the mirror on the bathroom door. The outdoor life at Shady Glen had given him a tan and firmed up some of that extra flab he had carried for years. He looked like a businessman in town for a night out. He smiled to himself. These wouldn't be his working clothes, this was just phase one.

The elevator was empty except for an oriental couple that was chattering away in some language that sounded like music notes to Roger. He smiled and motioned them out ahead of him as the elevator stopped at the lobby. He received smiles and bows in return.

Roger walked to the bar just off the lobby. He'd have one drink, then go out for a relaxing dinner at one of the waterfront restaurants. He sat on a stool and ordered a martini, up and very dry, from the bartender.

"Gin or Vodka?" asked the bartender.

"Absolute vodka, please, shaken, not stirred. I sound like James Bond, don't I?" Roger smiled at the bartender.

"Maybe, but that's the best way to make a martini. Hard to believe all the different ones out there now, everything from cosmopolitans to chocolate martinis."

The man behind the bar set up a glass with ice and a little water in it to chill, then poured a healthy shot of Absolute vodka into a shaker. He added ice and began shaking the concoction while he dumped the ice and water out of the glass. He splashed in a small amount of vermouth, rinsed it around, and then dumped it into the sink. He sat the chilled glass in front of Roger and poured in the vodka. A thin skim of ice floated on top. He speared two olives and added them to the ice-cold drink.

"Here you go, sir. One extra dry martini."

Roger took a sip, then gave the bartender a thumbs up. "Perfect."

"I see you've got a lot of homeless people around the area." Roger watched the bartender washing glasses.

"Yeah, more than our share." The bartender glanced up, a frown crossing his face. "There are more this year than last, and it seems like more moving in. I think it's because the city is so soft on them."

"How's that?" Roger asked.

"They've got all kinds of shelters and programs for them here. I think it just attracts more of them."

"Are there more in this area of town than elsewhere?" Roger kept his tone neutral, as if he were just making conversation.

"Just during the tourist season. They don't hang around here at night, though, they congregate in a lot of the parks at night, take Golden Gate park, for instance, lots of places for them there to hide out. It seems to be the most popular."

"Too bad," Roger changed the subject, "Hey, how about them Giants?"

They chatted for a while longer, until the bartender got busy with some other customers.

Roger sat on the stool and nursed the martini, watching the crowd in the bar. Several tables had customers looking at brochures. There must be some convention in town. That was good. He'd be less likely to be noticed, although that wasn't really a concern this trip. Roger enjoyed the first martini, and had another.

The bar mix of peanuts and Chex in the little dishes went well with the martinis.

This was just the first phase; he could relax for a while. Tomorrow, he would begin his search in earnest. He might make more trips to San Francisco to complete his project.

Roger paid for his drinks and left the bar. He had parked the Explorer in the garage under the motel. He left it there. He was within walking distance of the waterfront. The night was fairly mild and it was good to get out and stretch his legs.

He picked a restaurant that overlooked the bay and got a table with a good view. He ordered the surf and turf dinner, it was about time he enjoyed some of the money he had accumulated. He had a couple of glasses of wine with the dinner and finished up with tiramisu and coffee.

Roger left the restaurant and walked back along the waterfront. He passed the turnaround for the cable cars and went across the street to the Buena Vista bar for an Irish coffee. He had counted ten panhandlers on his walk around the area.

The bar was crowded and noisy. Roger got a seat at the far end of the bar and placed his order. He watched the bartender line up a row of coffee cups, drop sugar cubes in them, then pour coffee in a steady stream down the row of cups, followed by Jameson's Irish whiskey, with whipped cream on top. It was like a production line. The brochure on the bar claimed they poured up to two thousand a day.

He nursed his coffee and watched the crowd. Mostly young office types. They had shed their suit coats and donned windbreakers. The women were still in their dresses from work. Everybody was laughing and having a great time. Roger smiled at them. *Must be nice to lead such a normal life.* he thought.

All the gaiety was beginning to depress him, so he left the Buena Vista and headed back towards his hotel. On each corner, homeless men shook syrofoam cups at him, "Any change, mister?"

Roger ignored their question, but gave each a close look. None met his criteria.

CHAPTER 38

Roger slept until nine that morning. He hadn't done that in a long time. He got up, showered, shaved and dressed in some jeans and sneakers. He pulled a sweatshirt over his head. It was probably still cool outside. He helped himself to the complimentary Danish and coffee in the lobby and picked up a handful of tour guides and maps at the front desk. His best hunting area would be the tourist spots.

Roger was looking for another identity. Recent events had unnerved him. It had been a good idea to have an emergency bolthole. He wanted a fairly good I.D., preferably a drivers license, something that he could use, if only temporarily. The Richard Whiteman identity had fit like a glove. He had the background info, the looks, age, everything. He'd be more than lucky to get another that good. If he could get something for an emergency, something that would last for a short time, he could always go on the hunt for a better one. He wanted something as a backup in case things got too hot too quick for the Richard Whiteman he had gotten used to.

A homeless person would be less likely to be missed, and less likely to have close relatives looking for him. He sure wouldn't be a loss to the community. Roger thought he would be doing the city of San Francisco a favor to reduce the homeless population by one. He smiled to himself at the thought.

The problem, as he saw it, lay in getting rid of the body. There was always a chance another homeless person would recognize a body if it turned up. It was a small chance, for sure, as he couldn't see one of them filing a missing persons report, or talking to the police. Still, it would be better if the body disappeared entirely, like Richard Whiteman had.

Roger got on the Powell-Hyde cable car and rode it down to Chinatown. He stepped off of the car and started walking towards downtown, keeping his eyes open for likely targets. There were enough of them. Almost every street had one or two panhandlers with their Styrofoam cups, looking for change.

Roger couldn't figure out how to approach them. He dropped some change in a cup, but the wretch holding it never looked at him, just a mumbled "Thanks, man." When Roger tried to talk to him, the man shuffled off, pushing a grocery cart full of rags.

He'd have to find a different strategy. He had time; he was just feeling his way along for now. He'd go back and get the car and start exploring different areas of the city. He had as long as it took.

CHAPTER 39

Fred Jackson didn't feel he was that different from the rest of the residents in San Francisco. He was as much a part of the city as the buildings and parks he stayed in. He felt nearly invisible, people walked past him, rarely even looking directly at him. If they did look, it was either with anger, or pity, or sometimes fear. In his own mind, he was a survivor, a tough, clever individual that could get by on nearly nothing.

Indeed, he had nothing. No bank account, no wardrobe, no kitchen cupboards loaded with foodstuffs. What he had, he wore, or carried in his pockets, the ones without holes in them. His meals were generally something he scrounged for, picking up cans and bottles for the deposit, once in a while making a score for some pocket change.

He still had his old DD-214 from his discharge. That and his I.D. card took care of his medical needs and sometimes got him a place to stay overnight. They were getting on to him at the Vets hospital. He had a hard time convincing them he was sick anymore. Especially when he still smelled from the wine and beer he had consumed.

He had cashed in enough cans and bottles to get a three-dollar pitcher at the Corner Tap. It was a good time to go there, it would be crowded and sometimes he could pick up tips and change off the bar when the bartender was busy. It was just late enough that some of the customers would be feeling the booze, maybe get a little careless.

He looked at his reflection in a storefront window as he headed to the bar. Not too bad, he had a dark shirt on with a jacket he had picked up at the mission. His pants had a few stains, but if he got up close to the bar, nobody would notice. Luckily, he had shaved yesterday after he got his soup. They always had some disposable razors and soap in the john at the mission. He brushed a hand over the bristle on his face. He'd be o.k.

The smell of spilled beer and cigarette smoke hit him when he pushed into the bar. He breathed deep, relishing the second hand smoke. There was an empty stool near the end of the bar. He worked his way towards it, pushing through the crowd standing around the happy hour snacks of chips and peanuts. He'd hit that after he had his place at the bar. There was a ball game on the TV; the Giants were playing at home. Most of the patrons were watching the game, yelling their encouragement.

He sat on the stool and slid his glance up and down the bar. Lots of goodies there. Change, packs of cigarettes, all carelessly laying on the bar top. The bartender stopped and gave him a suspicious look.

"Gimme a pitcher" He laid his three dollar bills on the bar.

169

The bartender looked from him to the money, then came back with a small pitcher of beer and a glass. He took the money without a word and went to answer another yell for more beer.

Fred poured some beer into the glass and sat it on the bar to declare his space. He walked over to the snack table and filled two paper plates with chips and peanuts. He shuffled back to the bar and sat his plates on either side of his beer, as close to the change lying on the bar as he could. He'd have to watch for his chance.

God. That beer tasted good! It would be hard to make it last, he wanted to gulp it down. He snacked on some peanuts and looked around the bar. Nobody was paying him any attention except for that old guy sitting against the wall. He kept glancing his way. No matter, he wouldn't be any problem, probably just snuck out of the house for a quick one. He looked like a hen-pecked husband.

Fred took another sip of his beer. The man next to him was watching the game. There was a fiver on the bottom of his change sitting next to Fred's peanuts. He'd keep an eye on that. He had some chips, then took another small sip of beer.

About that time somebody hit a long ball on the TV. Everybody turned toward the set. Fred slipped the five out from under the ones and palmed it as he turned toward the TV on the wall. All eyes were on the TV, except for that old guy. He was looking at Fred.

Fred met his eyes for a second, then turned back towards his beer. *Wonder if he saw me?* He made a quick glance back, but the old guy was looking at the TV. *Whew. Thought I'd had it there!* Fred thought to himself.

The noise died down for a second, and the crowd started refueling between innings. The guy next to him ordered another drink, and didn't even notice he was five short. The

Don't Talk to Strangers

barkeep took some bills from his stack and sat his drink down in front of him.

He took a big swig of the drink and turned back towards the TV. The bartender moved on down the line.

Fred sipped at his beer. He had slipped the five into his shirt pocket. Things were looking good tonight. He glanced to his left. Just some coins on that side. He could wait. He poured some more beer into his glass and went back to the table for more chips and peanuts. The old guy was looking at him again. Gave him the creeps.

Back at the bar, his neighbor on the left ordered a round for him and his buddy and laid a twenty on the bar. The barkeep brought the drinks and laid the change down next to them. Another fiver on the bottom.

Fred kept nursing his beer, waiting for another good play on the TV. It came at the bottom of the ninth. Marquis Grissom hit a home run. The crowd went wild, yelling and cheering. Fred palmed the five without a problem. It went into his shirt pocket with the other. He turned towards the TV and scanned the cheering mob in the bar. The old guy was looking at him again. He had to have seen Fred palm the five. Then he half smiled and turned to look at the TV. Fred was getting the willies.

Fred finished his snacks and poured the last of the beer into his glass. He was getting out of here while he was ahead. The game would be over soon, and the bar would quiet down anyway. The old guy was freaking him out. He gulped down the beer and slid off the barstool. He watched the old guy out of the corner of his eye as he slipped to the door. He was just sitting there, watching the TV.

Fred got outside and headed towards the corner. He could stop in the all night quick shop and get a bottle of wine with the money he had picked up. A pack of cigarettes too. He'd take it back to his spot in the park. Party time tonight.

CHAPTER 40

Roger watched the wretch slide out the door. Sneaky one. This guy fit his criteria, even closer than he had hoped. He gave him enough time to get outside, then left a bill on the table and followed. It had turned dark since he had first gone in the bar. Fog was creeping in from the bay and left halos around the streetlights.

The homeless man was just turning the corner at the end of the street when Roger stepped outside. He followed from a safe distance, keeping in the shadows. He had watched him from the moment he came into the bar. He had seen him swipe the change from the guys on either side of him. It appeared he had had plenty of practice. The worn clothes and day old beard had given him away. He was probably headed for the nearest liquor store to spend his ill-gotten gain.

Roger was right. He was going in the all night liquor and deli in the middle of the block. Roger waited in a doorway across the street. It wasn't long until his target came out, lighting a cigarette and carrying a brown paper bag. He worked with the top of the bag, then raised it to his lips and took a long drink of whatever was in it. He coughed, spit, and smiled to himself. He stuck the cigarette in his mouth and headed on down the street.

They were walking west on Balboa Street. Roger had scouted the area earlier. There were all kinds of brochures available about the San Francisco homeless. He knew from his talk with the bartender at the hotel that west of here was the Golden Gate Park, a hangout for homeless people. They would hike back into the woods to camp, or some would bed down in the damp, chilly caves near the old Sutro baths. Regardless of where, it would probably be isolated. His man wouldn't want to share his hard-earned booze.

They crossed over to Fulton Street and continued west, the bum tipping the bottle frequently. By the time they reached the eastern end of the park, the derelict was starting to weave a little. He was on his fourth cigarette. Roger still followed at a distance, although the man wouldn't have noticed if he were right behind him.

They came to an entrance of Golden Gate Park and the now inebriated man swerved in, stumbling over a crack in the pavement. Roger followed him a little closer now. He obviously had a destination in mind, as he cut off of the road and followed a well-worn path into the timber. They walked on, deeper into the trees, the target still nipping at the bottle.

Finally, they came to a small clearing. A ragged lean-to was in the middle, with empty cans and bottles scattered around. Rags covered the floor of the lean-to. The fog had cleared and a bright moon shone down on the forest floor, lighting it with a pale luminescence. Roger hung back in the shadows. He'd wait for the man to finish the bottle.

The drunk knelt down by a rock fire ring. There was the rustling of paper then light as he started a small fire in the ring. He added some sticks, then a few larger branches as they caught.

Suddenly, there was movement on the other side of the clearing. A figure stepped out from behind a tree.

"Whatcha got, Fred?" a raspy voice called out.

Another homeless man, dressed in old stained dress pants and a t-shirt, covered with a hooded sweatshirt. He was bearded and looked dirty and unkempt. He wore old running shoes with no socks, his dirty ankles showing above the shoe tops.

"Fuck off, Sailor," Fred responded, clutching the bottle to his chest.

"Hey buddy, that's no way to talk to your best friend." Sailor whined back, "How about a little snort for old times sake?" Sailor reached out towards Fred.

"Ain't enough left to share, so fuck off!" Fred tipped the bottle once again, and reached into his shirt pocket for a cigarette. He stuck a cigarette in the corner of his mouth, and held the bottle under one arm as he struck a match to light up.

"Damn! Cigarettes too? You really hit it big time tonight." Sailor exclaimed, stepping closer to Fred. "Gimme a cig, buddy, you can spare one'a them." Sailor had his hand out, reaching towards Fred.

Fred clutched the bottle again. "Awright, you mooching bastard, one cigarette." Fred pulled out the pack and flipped one out towards Sailor.

Sailor caught it in the air, cradling it as though it were precious. "How 'bout a light?"

179

Roger watched this exchange with fascination. These two creatures from another world were behaving in a manner he had never seen before. Their whole lives were focused around a bottle of booze and some cigarettes. No lofty goals for them.

Sailor had his cigarette going now, sucking in the smoke with obvious relish.

"God, this is good, first whole unused cig I've had in a week!" He eyed the bottle in Fred's hand. "I'd sure go for a nip a that hooch."

"Fuck off, dammit." Fred turned, hiding the bottle with his body. He took a step back.

"One fuckin drink you miserable prick." Sailors face contorted in anger. "One drink is all I want!" He held his hand out towards Fred; it was shaking with desire and anger.

Fred clutched the bottle with his left hand, the right balled up into a fist. "I'll give you one punch if'n you don't fuck off."

As Sailor lunged forward, Fred swung his fist in a short arc and caught him on the side of the head, knocking Sailor to the ground. The force of the swing, and the amount of hooch he had already drunk, left Fred staggering towards the lean-to.

Sailor was on his hands and knees, shaking his head, a grim look of determination on his face. His right hand was resting on one of the rocks that made up the fire ring by the lean-to. He picked it up and lunged at Fred, swinging the rock at his head. It connected with a loud smack. Fred staggered forward a few steps and fell face down into the lean-to, knocking it over. The bottle slid from his hand to the ground, falling on its side.

Sailor tossed the rock aside and grabbed the bottle, turning it upright before too much of the precious fluid could run out. Fred forgotten, he tipped the bottle up to his mouth.

Roger could see his throat working as he chugged down the liquor. He mentally gagged at the thought of that cheap booze burning down Sailors throat. Sailor didn't bat an eye, just kept chugging.   Finally, he lowered the bottle, belched, and coughed a hacking cough. Fred hadn't moved. Sailor hunted the ground for his lost cigarette, found it, and stuck it back in his mouth. He took a deep drag, then coughed and hacked again for another long minute. Finally, he walked over to where Fred lay. He turned him over with his foot and started going through his pockets. He found the change in Fred's shirt pocket and stuck it in his pants. He helped himself to Fred's cigarettes and matches too. There was a bloody smear on the side of Fred's face, his mouth hung open. Sailor stood up, looked around and slipped into the trees opposite the side where Roger hid behind a large pine. Just before disappearing into the trees, he tipped the bottle once more and threw the empty container back at Fred.

Roger waited behind the tree for a good five minutes. Then he cautiously approached Fred. He could hear his raspy breathing as he stepped into the clearing. Fred was unconscious, either knocked out from the blow, or passed out from the booze. Sailor had probably taken the only thing Roger wanted, Fred's I.D., if he had one. He knew the city had programs for the homeless, and they had cards for them to use at various places for food and clothing. That was Roger's hope, something that would give him another name.

He went through Fred's pockets. Sailor had cleaned out the shirt pocket. The pants pockets had large holes in them, which explained why Fred had put everything in his shirt pocket. He was about to give up when he noticed a string tied around the worn cracked belt at Fred's waist. It went over the belt and inside the waistband of Fred's pants.

Roger pulled the string and found it was tied to a sock. He gingerly opened the smelly sock and dumped the contents on the ground. There were some papers in a zip lock plastic bag, along with some change and a five-dollar

183

bill. Must be Fred's emergency stash. There was also a fair size folding knife. Sailor might have been lucky to get the telling blow in. Roger had no doubt that Fred would have used the knife.

He opened the zip lock bag and studied the papers. There was a DD-214 from the Navy, with the service dates for a Fred Jackson. There was a card from the VA hospital, and an expired California driver's license. Bingo! Roger stuffed the papers back into the plastic bag and put them in his jacket pocket. Now, what to do with poor old Fred?

Roger studied the body lying on the ground. Fred would probably at least report the lost papers to the Veterans Administration. Too bad Sailor hadn't hit him a little harder, chances were that he would have eventually been found and chalked up to another homeless death. Maybe he should rectify Sailors oversight. The rock was lying where Sailor had dropped it. Roger picked it up and weighed it in his hand.

Fred snored on, oblivious to his impending demise.

He kneeled down by Fred's body. Roger turned Fred's head so that the mark left by Sailors smash was facing up. He took the rock and raised it over his head.

Just then, some sixth sense must have aroused Fred. His eyes blinked open and he turned just as Roger brought the rock smashing into his head. The rock caught Fred right between the eyes. Blood spurted out Fred's nose. He let out a choked gurgle and Roger hit him again, this time on the side of the head where Sailors first blow had landed. Fred's eyes rolled up into his head and a long sigh escaped his lips. Roger raised the rock and crashed it into Fred's head again. Fred jerked and shook and finally lay still.

Roger caught his breath and watched Fred for any sign of life. The snoring had stopped and he didn't move. Roger felt his neck for a pulse. Nothing there. He just looked at

Fred for a while. This had been much easier than Richard. He felt no remorse at all. He had done the city a favor, ridding it of one of its parasites. A year ago, he would have stopped his car, rather than hit a squirrel running across the street. Now, he had a body count of four.

Roger didn't analyze his feelings. He just felt that this was justified. He needed another I.D., Fred wasn't reaching any great potential with his, so why shouldn't Roger? He really felt pretty good about this. His plans were going according to schedule.

He stood and looked around. It was dark and quiet around the campsite. The fire had died down and only a few flames flickered. It would be out soon. The scene was obviously one of a fight for the now empty liquor bottle. If anything, the cops would be looking for Sailor. If Sailor found the body first, he would probably believe he had killed Fred and be long gone before any police came around.

Roger backtracked out of the park and back towards the Corner Tap, where he had parked the Explorer. He made the return trip without incident. He stopped at the tavern and went to the restroom. The smell in the bathroom was about enough to knock you over. Roger checked his clothes for blood from Fred. There were a few dark spots on his jean leg. Roger wiped at them with a paper towel and got most of it off. Wouldn't matter, it didn't show up much on the dark jeans.

He ordered vodka on the rocks from the bartender. There must have been a shift change; a new man was behind the bar. His bald head glistened with sweat and from the overhead lights. He placed the drink in front of Roger and went back to washing glasses at the sink.

The crowd had mostly dispersed after the ball game. A few locals still sat around watching CNN on the TV. Roger finished his drink and went back to the Explorer. The fog was back, drifting in tendrils across the street. He'd finish his project tomorrow.

CHAPTER 41

Gary had made his decision. He was going to return to L.A. He wrote up an answer to the letter he had received from the department and asked for the necessary paperwork to apply for reinstatement. If they accepted his application, he would notify the city here of his decision and make arrangements to get back to California.

He finished the letter and walked over to the post office. He dropped the letter in the outgoing mail chute and immediately felt better. This is what he needed to do. It felt so good to make the move. He had been worrying over it for weeks. Now that he had decided, he felt as though a tremendous weight had been lifted from his shoulders. Now he would be anxious until he got his reply. He could only hope they still wanted him back.

CHAPTER 42

Roger woke from a deep sleep. He felt rested and refreshed. The hard part was done, now he would finish his contingency plans and head back to Oregon. He rolled out of the bed and took a long hot shower. He shaved and dressed in his wash pants and a clean shirt. It was Saturday morning, the restaurant at the hotel was crammed full of weekend patrons. Roger headed out to the street. He'd have breakfast at one of the many coffee shops, and then get to work.

It was a beautiful, sunny day. Roger walked towards the Marina and stopped at a sidewalk coffee bar. He had coffee and a muffin at one of the stand-up tables by the sidewalk. He watched the people going past, all wrapped up in their weekend plans, sightseeing and enjoying the San Francisco waterfront. Roger had other plans.

He went back to the hotel and caught a cab. He had the driver take him towards the airport, then pull over at one of the many used car lots in South San Francisco. He paid off the driver and walked on to the lot. He had taken $2,000 from his stash fund just for this purpose. He walked around the lot, looking at mid-size sedans in his price range. He hadn't walked ten feet when a salesman appeared at his elbow.

"Hi there, looking for a good used car?" The man had a red face, with freckles, a huge smile and a mop of red hair. He wore a gaudy plaid jacket that would never button over the stomach that protruded over the top of his pants.

"Yes, I'm looking for a car for the wife to use while I'm at work." Roger had his spiel memorized. "Just something she can drive to the grocery and shopping, nothing fancy."

"I've just been promoted, and I'll be working at a different office. I've lived down the street from work for the last ten years. I'm going to have to start driving to work. I haven't had to drive and she's been keeping the car. That's all going to change now."

Roger had left the sport jacket and was wearing a windbreaker with his slacks and shirt. He hoped he looked like a blue-collar worker and a native. He planned to pay cash for whatever he found, and drive it to a secure spot where he could access it easily.

"We've got just what you want, you just pick out the exact model you want. You looking for a compact, a full size, or a mid size?" The salesman was eager to help.

"I think a mid size, something like maybe a Camry."

"You're in luck. We've got five Camry's in stock, from a pre-owned 1986, up to a last years' model. What price range you looking at?"

"I want a good reliable model, clean, without a lot of miles on it. Not too new, can't

afford that. Something under two thousand."
Roger felt he had the upper hand. If this dealer
didn't work out, there were three more within
walking distance.

"I've got just what you're looking for."
The salesman took Roger by the elbow and led
him to a light blue car towards the back of the
lot. "Here's a 1990 model, automatic, air, full
power, stereo. It belonged to a local teacher.
She traded up to a newer model just last week.
We were going to send this to the auction, but
haven't got around to it yet."

There was a test drive, a little haggling
on the price, and then Roger made his pitch.

"I'll pay you the price in cash, if you can
let me drive it out today. I might need a
temporary plate. My driver's license is expired,
wife's been doing all the driving, she's working
today, so I'd have to drive it home. I'm getting
my license renewed Monday. Will that be a
problem?"

Roger had the wad of bills in his hand. The salesman looked from Roger to the bills and back, he was having a hard time to keep his mouth from watering. "Nothing we can't handle. Let's fill out the papers, and I'll see what I can do to get you in the drivers seat today."

Another half-hour and two hundred dollars over the asking price, and Roger drove out of the lot in his Camry. He headed towards the long-term lots at the San Francisco airport.

Roger parked the Camry and hid the keys on top of the right rear wheel. It should be fine for at least three months. He had a dealer plate on it now, but he would switch plates if he needed to drive the car out. He had stashed another $5,000 under the back seat. The Fred Jackson ID was in the glove box. He was set.

Roger took the shuttle to the airport and caught a cab back to his hotel. He checked out and got back in the Explorer.

194

Don't Talk to Strangers

Chapter 43

Roger was at Twin Pines, deep into an article in the paper about gardening. It would soon be time to start getting his plot ready for planting in the spring. He didn't notice Gary slide into the booth opposite him. He jumped when Gary spoke.

"Hey Dick, what's got you so engrossed?" Gary leaned back in the seat, his hands folded on the tabletop.

"Oh, hi Gary, just reading about how to get your garden ready for planting in the spring. You have to get the ground ready now, you know."

"No, I didn't, but if you say so." Gary paused, then continued, "Do you know a cop named Patterson in Winslow, Arizona?"

Roger's eyes widened. What was this?

195

"Yeah, I remember him. When I was in Winslow, he asked me some questions about a case up in Iowa. Where did you hear about him?"

"He called me about you." Gary said. "Something new came up on that old case. He tracked you down."

"Tracked me down. What in hell he want with me?" Roger was flustered; he thought this was all behind him.

"The bank that was robbed has been pushing on that case. They got some bad press, or something out of it. Seems like they tracked the killer over to Omaha. Some clerk at a motel there I.D.'d him from a picture they found in his apartment in Iowa. They took that picture to about all the motels in Omaha, I guess. Finally got a hit at a motel on the north side of town, near that Wal-Mart you worked at. An agent that worked the case in Iowa talked to a bartender near the motel. He verified the same picture. Said he remembered you, and thought

196

maybe you had talked to the suspect there in the bar." Gary was watching Roger across the table. "That agent would like to have a word with you. He got your address in Winslow and got in touch with Patterson, and Patterson called me. He got your forwarding address from the post office and asked if I knew you."

Roger's mind was running wild. Jesus! Not now, after all this time. What was he going to do? He tried to keep his expression unreadable. He put on his best poker face. He couldn't get Gary interested in this. Gary was a pro. He remembered the stories from the LAPD. He had to get this stopped before it went any further.

"Sure, but how am I going to do that? Who is he? I don't know how or who to get in touch with."

"Let's go over to the station, I'll give him a call. I've got his name and number from Patterson in Winslow."

Roger followed Gary's patrol car over to the station. He had to fight the urge to just get on the highway and take off. He had to get this under control, and fast. He parked next to Gary's car and followed him into the station. They walked back to Gary's office and Roger sat down while Gary closed the door after him. Gary walked around the desk to his chair and sat down.

"Give me a second to find his number here. His name is Rich Ramirez; he's an F.B.I. agent from the Des Moines field office. Hang on a sec, it's a 515 area code, let see, here it is." Gary picked up a post-it note and lifted the receiver from the phone. He dialed in the number and sat looking at Roger. Roger could hear the buzz of the phone on his side of the desk, then someone picked up on the other end. He could hear a voice, but couldn't make out the words.

"Yeah," said Gary, "This is Chief Frost at the Shady Glen PD, I talked to you earlier. I have Dick Whiteman here in the office. Hang on while I put you on speaker." Gary pushed a button on his phone and replaced the receiver. "Can you hear me o.k.?"

"Yeah", said the voice from the speaker, "I hear you fine."

"Great, Dick is right here, you can go ahead and ask your questions. We're in my office and it's private."

"Hello, Mr. Whiteman, my name is Rich Ramirez. I'm with the F.B.I. and we're looking into a case that started in Iowa. We're trying to track down a suspect and we have reason to believe you might have met him."

"I wish I could help," said Roger, "Gary told me about it, but I don't remember anybody particular from that night. After I got off work, I stopped in a couple of places and spoke to several people. I don't remember anybody specific, it's been a long time ago."

"I understand, Mr. Whiteman, I'm surprised the bartender even remembered. We're just trying to track down this Roger Wardlow. You don't happen to remember a name like that do you?"

It seemed strange hearing someone speak that name after so long. Roger had pushed it back; trying to hide it for so long, he thought maybe that name was gone and forgotten.

"No, it doesn't sound familiar. Like I said, I spoke to several people, some I'd seen before, and some I hadn't. I was celebrating my retirement all over. Lot of people spoke to me."

"I see, well, I'll send this picture of Wardlow out. Maybe you can recognize it and it might jog a memory. Don't know what good it will do, we're just trying to find out how he got out of town, which we're sure now that he did, maybe even that night." Ramirez sounded weary of the conversation, probably one of many he'd had already.

"That will be fine, I'll look at it, and if it rings a bell, I'll get back in touch." Roger was sweating now; he didn't want any pictures of him coming out. "Just send it to my post office box here. It's box 113 here in Shady Glen, zip code is 97555."

"O.k., I'll do that, and after you take a look at it, give it to the chief there, will you? He can send it back to me here." Ramirez was obviously disappointed he didn't get more, "I'll express it out today, and you should have it in a couple of days at the most. Be sure to get a good look at it."

"Sorry I couldn't be more help," Roger said. God! He had been afraid Ramirez was going to send it to Gary. He'd figure out a way to get rid of it.

"That's o.k., I really didn't expect much, but had to take a chance. Thanks for your time."

They said their good-byes and Gary cut the connection. He looked at Roger across the desk. "That was strange. Wonder how that bartender remembered after all this time."

Roger wondered too. Just his luck to run into somebody with a photographic memory. He had to make sure he got that picture and got rid of it before Gary asked about it.

"Well, guess I'll head back to Twin Pines and finish my paper. You coming?"

"No, I've got work to do here in the office. I'll catch you later." Gary remained seated at his desk. Roger could tell he was still thinking about the call.

Roger walked out to the Explorer. He still had the urge to run. That episode had scared him, more than he cared to admit. They must have got that picture of him and Marian they had taken in Las Vegas. It had been in the top drawer of the dresser when he took off that day. There would be no doubt it was him if anyone saw it.

Gary was the closest thing to a friend that Roger had ever had. His mother had always told him not to talk to strangers, but if you didn't talk to strangers, how would you make any friends?

Now was not a good time for Roger to be developing friendships. How could he? He had secrets he could tell no one. Anyone that knew his secrets wouldn't be a friend for long.

CHAPTER 44

Gary sat at his desk looking at the phone. Something there. He had that old feeling again, something wasn't quite right, but he couldn't put his finger on it. There was something else he should have asked Ramirez, but couldn't for the life of him figure it out. Strange, a case that far away and that long ago could stir up that old investigator feeling again.

He shrugged and pulled out a stack of paperwork. If it came to him, he'd act on it. Eventually, it would, it always did.

CHAPTER 45

The next day was a nightmare for Roger. He stopped at the post office four times, the last time, just as the window was closing. He caught the clerk just as he was pulling down the shutter to close up.

"Did you ever get that special letter for me?" Roger asked.

"No, and I'm not surprised, it almost always takes an extra day for an express to get here, too many connections involved. Check with me tomorrow. The guy that sent it can get his money back, the next day delivery is supposed to be guaranteed."

Roger could care less if Ramirez got his money back. He just didn't want that picture in the wrong hands. What if Ramirez had decided to send the picture to Gary instead of him? Or both of them? Maybe he should make plans to disappear.

His heart jumped into his throat as he started to leave the post office. Gary had just pulled in and parked next to his Explorer. He fought down the panic as Gary got out of the car and headed inside. Roger went to his box to keep from appearing too frightened as he heard Gary open the door to the post office.

"Hey Dick, you get that picture yet?"

Roger turned and forced a sickly smile, "Not yet, maybe Ramirez forgot."

"I doubt that, probably just our lousy mail service." Gary smiled, dropped some letters in the outgoing slot and turned back to the door. He paused with his hand on the door.

"It'll be interesting to see what that guy looks like, even more to see if you recognize him."

"Yeah, right, I doubt that." Roger closed the door to his post office box and followed Gary into the parking lot. They got into their separate vehicles and Gary drove out, back towards the police station. Roger sat there for a minute, calming his nerves. At least he knew Gary hadn't seen the picture. So far, anyway.

That night, Roger slept hardly at all. He tossed and turned, and finally got up and fixed a pot of coffee. He might as well stay up; he knew he wouldn't get any sleep until he had that picture. As he sat there, he thought about what he should do next. He got up and took the briefcase full of money from its hiding place under the sink in the dinette. He looked at it, then closed and locked It. For now, he'd carry it with him; just in case he had to take off in a hurry. He packed the old gym bag with a few clothes and an old travel kit. Better to be safe than sorry.

He was waiting in the lot when the post office opened that morning. He watched each car coming in; terrified that Gary would show up. When the clerk opened the door, Roger was the first inside.

"Got your express mail this morning." The clerk grinned at Roger, "Day late, dollar short." He went into the workroom and came back with a large blue and white envelope. "Sign here, and it's all yours." He held out the envelope and a pen and pointed to the signature line on the envelope. Roger signed it, and the clerk took his copy and handed back the envelope. Roger took it and nearly ran from the post office. He checked the lot one more time then got in the Explorer and drove out to the highway. He wanted to be alone for a while.

He drove north, finally pulling in at the fish hatchery. There were no other cars in the lot this early. The hatchery appeared deserted; nobody was around the ponds where the fish were kept.

He ripped open the envelope and pulled out the picture and a sheet of paper. The picture

208

grabbed his attention first. It was as he thought, a copy of the picture from Las Vegas. Marian looked back at him from the picture, a smile on her face. Nothing like his last remembrance of her, crying and pulling on his arm; just before she went down the stairs. She looked happy, and his face in the picture wore a small bored smile.

The sheet was a short note from Ramirez, asking him to look at the picture and if he had any information or ideas at all, to call him collect. His phone number and address were at the bottom of the note. There was also a postscript to drop the picture off at Gary's office. Like he was about to do that.

Roger put the note and the picture back in the envelope. He drove to the picnic area of the hatchery and parked near one of the shelters. He took a pack of matches from the glove box and took the envelope to the small grill by the picnic tables. He was going to tear the picture up and burn the whole works, when an idea came to him.

He tore the picture into small pieces and burnt them in the grill. He kept the envelope with the note from Ramirez.

He got back in the Explorer and sat there for a while; pondering the story he would tell Gary. If Ramirez didn't send another picture to Gary, this just might work. There was no reason why he should. Finally, he put the car in gear and headed back to Shady Glen, the seeds of a plan starting to grow into an idea.

CHAPTER 46

Back at the trailer, Roger dug out the old papers and pictures he had saved from the storage shed in Winslow. He took the picture of Richard and his wife out and looked at it. If he got a copy made on plain paper, it would look about the same as the picture Ramirez had sent of him and Marian.

He drove back through Shady Glen, hoping against hope he wouldn't see Gary. The highway went right past the police station, but there was no sign of Gary's patrol car there. His old pickup was in the corner of the lot, so Gary must be out on patrol somewhere.

Roger kept on driving, one eye on the rearview mirror. Five miles out of town, he relaxed. Gary wouldn't be this far out of town. He had missed him.

He drove on into Medford without incident. He drove to the mall and went into a Kinko's. They had the coin operated copy machines in the lobby. He made a copy of the picture of Richard and Mary and put it in the envelope with the note from Ramirez. He walked out of Kinko's without exchanging a word with anyone.

CHAPTER 47

Gary put the phone back on the cradle. He had been trying to get in touch with Dick Whiteman all morning. The clerk at the post office had told Gary that Dick got the picture that morning, early. He had expected Dick to stop by and share any ideas with him. Something was up; he could feel it in his bones. *Maybe I ought to call Ramirez,* he thought, *maybe he'd have more info.*

Gary reached for the phone, then stopped. He'd had a call early that morning, a raccoon had gotten into a brawl with one of his constituents Boston Terrier. The feisty little terrier had treed the Raccoon, and the owner had called Gary to get rid of it. It had taken over an hour to get the coon out of the tree and into a live trap, then out along the river where he turned it loose. Possibly, Dick had come by while he was playing game warden. He decided

213

to head to Twin Pines. If Dick hadn't showed up by the time he got back, he'd make that call to Ramirez. He might be able to save a long-distance call.

CHAPTER 48

An hour after he left Kinko's, Roger was back in Shady Glen. As he drove into town, he spotted Gary's patrol car at Twin Pines. He pulled into the lot and parked next to it.

Gary was sitting in a booth by the window.

"Hi, Gary." Roger slid in across from him, "I've been looking for you. I've got that picture from Ramirez. He wanted me to give it to you after I looked at it."

"Hey Dick, I just called you to see if you had it. Did it ring any bells for you?" Gary reached over and took the offered envelope from Roger.

"Not for me. Guy sure doesn't look like a killer, let alone a bank robber."

"They seldom do, not the good ones." Gary looked at the picture. "Nope, he sure doesn't. Wonder what tripped his trigger?"

"I wouldn't have a clue, Gary, that's your job. Figuring out what makes them tick. Don't think I could handle a job like that. You'd get where you didn't trust anybody."

Roger waved at Donna, and made a sipping motion. She nodded and headed for the coffeepot. He folded his arms and leaned on the tabletop.

"How do you go about catching somebody like that, Gary?"

"Usually, they catch themselves." Gary took a sip of coffee while holding the picture in his other hand. "they get overconfident, or screw up, or try it again. Rare one indeed that does one job and quits. We always get them in the end."

Wanna bet? Roger thought as he smiled at Gary across the table.

CHAPTER 49

Gary sat at his desk, looking at the picture. He'd send Ramirez an email and let him know he had the picture. He put the picture back in the folder and tossed it in his in-basket. He'd mail it later. This was a strange one. It was rare to get new info like this on an old case. He envied Ramirez. He liked working cold cases. When you broke one of those, it really gave you a good feeling. Ramirez seemed to have the same attachment. He looked forward to talking to him again.

This Wardlow guy seemed to have dropped off the face of the earth. That just didn't happen. There had to be a link somewhere. This guy had killed two people, robbed a bank, and then just disappeared. Sure, he had picked up a pretty good chunk of change in the robbery, but still, you couldn't just disappear. There had been no credit card charges, no contacts, nothing.   How did somebody just disappear?

Gary thought back over the cases he had worked in L.A.   Most of those were either crimes of passion, or smash and grab, drug related.   Once in a great while, he got a really deep crime, like a serial killer.   Those were the ones that really grabbed you.   Those guys were out for the glory, for the most part.   They had a twist in their psych that not only enjoyed the crime, but they got pleasure from challenging the police, and usually focused on a particular investigator.   It got to be a contest between the investigator and the instigator.   The odds were always in favor of the police, but sometimes, it played out too long.   Too many victims, too much of a contest.   That's what had burnt him out.   The last case had gone about two victims too many.   Gary had lost it.   He knew who the bastard was, but there was no evidence.   Gary had set him up, caught him at a crime scene by trickery and had blown him away.   Gary had created a scene that looked like a copycat killer.

His suspect always showed up at a crime scene like that, whether it was his or not. This time it had been his undoing. Gary had never been suspect. It was a clean scene. He was the only one that really knew what had transpired. Even though he justified it in his mind, he knew he had lost the contest. That was the beginning of the end of his career in LAPD. It was also the end of his marriage. He had been so focused on catching this asshole; he had ignored all the signs of the collapse of his marriage. Then he was wrapped up in self-analysis and guilt after. His wife had finally given up on him. It was all his fault. He knew it, and she knew it. She didn't really come down hard on him, she just walked away.

That was why he wanted to return to the LAPD. He felt he could put that ghost to rest. He'd find out soon enough, he had sent his papers in. Gary shook himself, back to the matter at hand.

He turned his attention to Ramirez' case. He wondered if this Wardlow character had planned all of this. The two victims were both the most likely he would have planned to get rid of if he had planned the robbery. They would have been the only ones that could call the law down on him immediately. He would have known there would be a lot of money that day. Maybe he had set up a phony I.D. somewhere and had the whole scene planned ahead of time.

On the other hand, if the two killings had been accidental, he probably had panicked and run. The big mystery was how he had disappeared. If this were his case, Gary thought he would check every flight, bus and train that had left Omaha for the week following the discovery of Wardlow's car in the parking lot. He had disappeared that same night, he had to have found transportation somehow. That would be the key that would unlock this one.

Gary was intrigued by this case. Nothing like this ever came up here at Shady

Glen. He looked at the clock. It was almost 4 o'clock. Six o'clock in Omaha. And it was Friday. He'd give Ramirez a call Monday; maybe they could hash it over and come up with something. He'd mail the picture back on the way home.

CHAPTER 50

That Sunday was Roger and Gary's fishing day. They used Gary's boat, pulling it with his pickup and putting it in the water upstream. They would fish their way down to the trailer park, then take Roger's Explorer back up to where Gary parked his pickup. They would drive both vehicles back to the trailer park and have lunch together.

Gary talked about the robbery and homicide while they fished. Roger tried several times to change the subject, but Gary seemed obsessed with it. The more Gary talked, the quieter Roger got. By the time they arrived at the trailer park, Roger was silent. Gary didn't seem to notice. As they drove back to Gary's pickup, Gary mentioned that he was calling Ramirez the next day.

"Isn't that a little extreme?" Roger asked. "I mean, do you think he'll even talk to you, being clear out here in Oregon and with no connection to the case?"

"I've told him about some of my cases from L.A. He's said that if I had any ideas, he'd be glad to hear them. They're pretty much at a dead end there in Omaha. I've got some ideas I want to run by him, see if they've tried all the leads. I used to be pretty good at tracking down people, if I do say so myself." Gary grinned at Roger. He was obviously hyped at getting back in the investigation business. "I've got some ideas on where he can take that picture."

Roger was sure his idyllic stay in Shady Glen was at an end. He figured he had maybe a week at best before Ramirez and Gary figured out what was happening. Ramirez would know as soon as he got the picture. It was time to move on. It would be time to use his new identity too. Richard Whiteman had served his purpose.

CHAPTER 51

After Gary left, Roger took stock of his options. They were limited. He would need an excuse to leave town. Some kind of emergency. He didn't want to give Gary an excuse to start tracking him right away. He needed to put some distance between himself and Shady Glen.

That evening, he called Gary.

"Hey Gary," he said when Gary answered his phone, "I've got to fly back to Kansas City for a couple of days. Mary's aunt died and I'm the only relative mentioned in her will. I used to stop by and see her when I was on the road. I guess she remembered that. I was wondering if you'd check on my trailer while I'm gone. I should be back by Friday, latest."

"Sure Dick, sorry about the aunt."

"Yeah, she was an old sweetheart. I used to take her out to eat when I was in the neighborhood. We always got along real good. She didn't have much, but they have to close the estate so they can settle it. It shouldn't take long, I've got to sign some papers and they want them as soon as possible."

"Not a problem. Anything else you need?"

"That should do it, just if you'd check out the trailer. You know where the spare key is, don't you?"

"Still keep it on the string tied to the propane tank?"

"Yep. I cleaned out the refrig and dumped the bread. That should be all that it needs, I'd just feel better knowing you'd keep an eye on it. I've got to catch that 6 a.m. flight in the morning from Medford."

"Sure thing. Have a good trip."

They chatted a little more. Then Roger hung up and started getting ready. He packed his old small suitcase with a few clothes and left everything else. He had grown attached to his fishing gear, but dared not take it with him. He was going to be very mobile. He already had his money case hidden under the back seat of the Explorer.

He emptied the refrigerator and bread into a garbage bag. He checked around for anything else. He'd take the papers and pictures of Richard with him. He'd dispose of them after he was away from here. He put the garbage in the dumpster and loaded his suitcase in the Explorer. He'd have to leave early in the morning. He called United Airlines and got flight reservations to Kansas City. He wanted to be covered, just in case.

At five the next morning, he drove through town and stayed on the highway as far as Medford. There he caught I-5 and headed south. He drove the rest of the day, getting into

San Francisco late in the afternoon. He got onto Interstate 80 and headed for the airport.

His Camry was in the same spot at the lot, covered with dust. He transferred his bags, and the money to the Camry. He left the Explorer in another spot. He took his parking chit with him to the Camry. He left the airport and went to a drive through car wash to remove the dust and dirt. He drove the Toyota to a motel that was near the airport and caught a cab back to the terminal.

He then proceeded to the ticket counter and bought a round trip ticket to Cancun, Mexico, using the Richard Whiteman I.D. and credit card. That ought to throw off any search for a while. He hit several ATM's; drawing out what cash he could until he reached his maximum on the Richard Whiteman bank account and credit card. No sense leaving good money.

He returned to the long-term parking lot. By now, it was approaching ten o'clock. The lot was nearly deserted. He took the plates from his Explorer and carried them with him to another car in the lot. There was no one around. The silence was eerie in the big garage. He swapped his plates with California ones. He realized that the plates would be reported stolen once the owner discovered the Nebraska plates. He went to another vehicle with California tags and swapped his set of California plates for another set. These probably wouldn't be noticed as soon as the Nebraska plates. He could replace the dealer sticker in the Camry with the new plates. It would buy him a little more time.

He caught a cab from the airport to the motel. He swapped the plates on the Camry and got back on interstate 80. He'd use the Fred Jackson ID for a while, even though it was pretty thin. It had served its purpose, getting him the car. After he had some miles between him and San Francisco, he could dump it. The expired drivers license would be more trouble than it was worth. He started driving east, going over his plan in his head. He had changed identities before, he was sure he could do it again. He had to find a suitable replacement for Richard Whiteman and Fred Jackson.

CHAPTER 52

Gary picked the phone up and dialed the Des Moines number from the post it note. He was in luck, Ramirez answered on the first ring.

"Ramirez," he said.

"Agent Ramirez, this is Chief Frost in Shady Glen, Oregon, do you remember me?"

"Sure, chief, I was going to give you a call today."

"I was wondering if you had that picture of that Roger Wardlow and his wife handy? Dick Whiteman brought the picture to me and I've got some ideas over the week-end."

Gary looked at the picture in his hand. He had cropped the wife out of the picture. He had enhanced it by scanning it into his computer and then made another copy of it with just the man, without the woman.

"First, let me email you back the changes I made to the picture. I think it will help with I.D.'s. I've got it on my computer here. What's your email address?"

"O.K., my email is rramirez@fbi.gov. I'm sitting at my computer right now."

"Hang on." Gary opened his email program and typed in the address. He attached the picture file and hit 'send'.

"I just sent it. I think this cropped version would work better, less distracting with the wife out of the picture. Once you get a look at it, I've got some other ideas for you, like emailing it around like I just did, and posting it to web pages for law enforcement. Also, you've got access to federal sites."

"Whoa, wait a minute Gary, you sent the wrong picture. This isn't Wardlow; this is a picture of Whiteman.   Where did you get a picture of Whiteman?"

"That's the one I got from Dick Whiteman, what do you mean, it was with your note."

"He must be pulling your leg, this picture is Whiteman's. Another thing, Richard Whiteman had a buddy here in Omaha that was holding some papers for him. Say's Richard wanted him to hang on to them until he got settled and had a regular mailing address. He says they're important stuff, like the title to his car and some insurance papers. He also says he hasn't ever heard from Whiteman. He turned up when I started asking around about Whiteman here on the case. I told him he was in Oregon. Wants to know if you'd have Whiteman give him a call."

Gary had a sudden sinking feeling in his stomach.   The strange feeling was growing stronger and taking form now for Gary.

"Do you have that picture of Wardlow on your computer?" Gary sat quietly at his computer.

"Yeah, just had it loaded on this morning. It's him and his wife together though, I didn't crop her out like you did in Whiteman's."

"Can you send it to me now?" Gary gave him his email address and waited while Ramirez typed in the message.

"It's on the way." Ramirez replied.

Gary watched as the picture formed on his screen, beginning at the top and unfolding down the screen. The feeling in his stomach gelled into a cold hand that wrenched his gut.

"Ramirez, I think we got a problem." Gary was looking at the picture that was supposed to be Roger Wardlow and was looking at the face of the man he knew as Richard Whiteman.

234

They put out a national APB for a pickup and hold for Roger Wardlow, AKA Richard Whiteman.

CHAPTER 53

Roger drove until he was nearly exhausted. He had taken interstate 80 east out of San Francisco. The lack of sleep the night before had taken its toll on him. He pulled into a rest area and parked at a dark spot away from the restrooms. He tilted the seat back and leaned back, sleep taking him almost immediately.

Roger didn't sleep well. Dreams and nightmares kept jerking him awake. Finally, about three in the morning, he went to the restroom, splashed some cold water on his face, and got back behind the wheel. He drove on through the rest of the morning bypassing Sacramento, and finally pulled into a Super 8 motel in Sparks, Nevada, just outside of Reno. He waited until the man at the counter was busy with customers checking out and managed to get a room paying cash putting a phony name and address on the registration.

He went to the room, showered, and flopped on the bed, wearing only his underwear, with his suitcase and money beside him. He planned on a short nap, but ended up sleeping poorly until six the following morning, nightmares waking him wide eyed and shaking through the night.

The sun was bright and hurt his eyes. He walked across the street to a Perkins and had breakfast. He would keep heading east after he finished eating. He walked back to the motel and got his bags and loaded them in the Camry. He left the room key on the desk in the room. He was nervous and pale when he got in the car.

CHAPTER 54

Gary put the phone back in the cradle. He had just talked to his new boss at LAPD. It was done; he was going back to L.A. He would meet with the mayor and city council tonight here in Shady Glen and tell them of his decision. It wasn't a big secret, he had already told them he was considering a move back to the LAPD, this would just make it official.

The case with Richard Whiteman had really clinched the deal. It had stirred up the old feelings of being on the hunt. He and Ramirez had made several phone calls, exchanging ideas. The FBI had an agent come down from Portland and he and Gary had gone through Roger's/Richard's trailer. They had found little in the way of leads. Roger had disappeared again.

Gary had received a commendation from the FBI for his assistance on the case. The FBI had seized Roger's trailer and had it stored at a compound in Medford. It was as though Roger had never been in Shady Glen, although there was still a lot of talk and supposition at Twin Pines. Donna had been pretty shaken when she found out. She had been questioned extensively by the FBI, but she didn't really have anything much to offer. She and Gary had discussed Roger in detail, but neither had any idea where he might have gone.

"I just can't see Dick, er Roger, or whatever his name is, committing murder." Donna said to Gary, her eyes still moist from the tears that came every time she thought of him.

"I know, it's tough to believe. I'll have to admit, I did have a few moments when I felt as though he was talking as though he was reading lines." Gary had his hand over Donna's, and patted it reassuringly. "It just

239

goes to show you, you can't judge a book by it's cover."

CHAPTER 55

Roger had been wandering around the west for a week. He was sure he had been missed in Shady Glen by now. Gary probably had the picture from Ramirez and they were now looking for Richard Whiteman and him. Too bad, that had been a good life; he had come so close to making it work.

He was using the Fred Jackson driver's license and hadn't had a problem with it so far. He got a few comments about it being a California license, but no one had noticed that it was expired, at least, so far.

Roger did a Google search on the homeless from his laptop. California seemed to have more than their share. The Golden Gate Park in San Francisco was mentioned as well as Pershing Square and Hollywood in Los Angeles as being favorite areas. The Golden Gate Park had worked well. Maybe he should try Pershing Square or Hollywood.

He left for Denver on a Wednesday morning. He drove to Ogallala and then took interstate 25 into Denver. He was paying cash for everything and using the Fred Jackson I.D. only when absolutely necessary. He was looking over his shoulder every minute, positive he would see Gary Frost coming after him.

He checked into a small Best Western motel in Denver. His fear that he had been tracked to San Francisco had made him worry about the California tags on his car. That evening, he drove the long drive to DIA, Denver International Airport, or "Dead in the Air" as it was referred to by the locals. He drove into the long-term parking and found a Ford Taurus at the edge of the lot. He quickly removed the plates, then drove to another isolated spot and changed those plates with another set on a dark blue Corolla, both being Colorado plates. The second set he put on his car. They should be o.k. for now. He felt better once he had changed away from the California tags. He didn't plan on staying in Denver very long.

CHAPTER 56

The young rookie policeman stood between the two women at the site of the minor fender-bender he had been called to. They were both talking at once and pointing fingers at each other.

"All right ladies, it really doesn't matter much who was at fault, your insurance companies will settle this incident. You've both done all that's required of you and the companies will settle your claims. It's really just a minor accident. Both cars are drivable and nobody was hurt, that's the main thing. I need to get your information for the accident report so you can file your claims and get your cars repaired. I'll need the registration and your driver's licenses so I can do the paperwork. You can just wait in your cars for a few minutes and I'll have the reports done."

The women glowered at each other and stomped off to sit in their cars. The rookie took the paperwork to his unit and called in the plate numbers, along with the DL's. While he waited for the call back, he started filling out the report. He was just about done, when the radio squawked to life, calling his unit number.

"Unit 27, I need a confirmation on the license of the Blue Corolla."

"10-4, base, F-Frank, G-George, X-X-ray, fiyuv, niner, four." He repeated the license number and put the mike back on the hook. He started filling out the last of the report.

"Unit 27, that number does not correspond to the vehicle registration. There is an outstanding warrant for unpaid parking for that license number. Please check and confirm."

The rookie looked at the paperwork on his clipboard. The number of the plate did not

245

match the number on the registration. "What the hell?" he thought.

He walked over to the blue Corolla. "Ma'am, how long has your car been parked at the airport?" he asked.

"I've just spent a week in California, visiting my mother." The woman responded, "Why, what's wrong?"

"I think somebody has switched plates with you" the rookie said, "I'll call it in."

"Base, this is unit 27, I think somebody has switched plates on this vehicle." He checked the plate number on the registration again, "You'd better put out a BOLO for this number. C-Charles, E-Edward, F-Foxtrot, seven, seven, niner. Colorado plate."

CHAPTER 57

Roger checked out of the Best Western the next morning and headed west. He had decided that Los Angeles would be a good place to hunt. According to a website he had visited, Los Angeles had over 91,000 homeless people, the largest of any metropolitan area in the country. That would give him a large group to work on. He was going to need a good solid identity that he could live with for awhile.

He took Interstate 70 west then caught I-15 out of Cove Fort, Utah. He spent the night in Cedar City, still in Utah, then started again in the morning.

He stopped at a motel just on the edge of Las Vegas. It wasn't much of a place, but there was a dining room and lounge attached. He got a room on the inner court and went directly to his room. He needed a few hours to catch up. He fired up his laptop and checked around his favorite sites, looking for anything relating to his latest moves.

Time to add to his stash in Vegas. He wanted to be sure he had a safe hideaway if things got worse.

He got his suitcase from the storage unit in Las Vegas and took it with him to his motel. He transferred $75,000 into his stash and rented another storage shed near the airport. He felt better with getting some of the cash in a safe place. It was just about split now between what he carried with him and what he had stashed. He used his combination padlock again and rented the unit for 6 months. This facility used the same procedure as the other had. Once he was signed up, he was given a code to open the outer gate and then he could drive right to his unit. He had used the Fred Jackson ID to rent this one. It was such a common name, he felt confident that it would be safe to use. Now he had his emergency backup secured.

He would head for L.A. tomorrow.

CHAPTER 58

Gary had his pickup packed with his books and clothes that he thought he might need in L.A. He would take I-5 south to Los Angeles. He'd probably have to spend one night on the road, he had gotten a late start, due to the extensive good-by's he'd made around Shady Glen. He didn't really mind, he didn't have to report until a week from this coming Monday. He'd move his stuff into his apartment in L.A. this weekend and re-acquaint himself with the city. He would be working out of the Central Bureau on east 6th street. He was familiar with the area. He liked being in downtown L.A. Close to the jewelry district, Chinatown, Little Tokyo and the financial district. It was a fascinating part of town. He was really looking forward to it. His apartment was just on the north side of the downtown area, actually within walking distance. It would serve him until he found something a little further out.

His group would be working the cold cases of the homeless homicides. They had plenty of work. These were some of the hardest cases to resolve, and not the highest priority of the department. Not much glory in resolving the murder of a homeless person, as compared to the big names that came up on a daily basis. Like the saying goes, "A dirty job, but somebody has to do it." Gary figured it was probably a test of his abilities and to see how much he had lost in his time away. It was fine with him. He'd get his feet wet. He wanted a challenge anyway, that was why he had decided to come back.

He took I-5 south towards Sacramento. It was a pretty drive through the mountains of northern California. He pulled into a Best Western motel and checked in for the night. He'd hit the road early tomorrow and get into L.A. in good time.

When he checked in, he asked the clerk to see if he could find a room in a Best Western near the city center. The clerk found a vacancy at the Dragon Gate Inn on Hill Street. Gary pictured the address in his mind. It would be close to both his office and his apartment. He could stay there over the weekend and move into his apartment the following week when his lease began.

"That will be perfect. Book me in for tomorrow night for two nights." Gary thought that would give him enough time to get his apartment set up and move in. He could always check out early, or add more time if he needed to.

Gary wondered briefly about Roger Wardlow. He still thought of him as Dick Whiteman. He seemed to have dropped off the radar. His last talk with Ramirez was a week ago and they had no new leads. They thought he was possibly in Nebraska or Colorado somewhere. Ramirez was confident he'd turn up. Gary wasn't so sure. He didn't see Dick as a career criminal. In some ways, he hoped he'd never hear about him again.

CHAPTER 59

Roger was having breakfast at a truck stop in Barstow. The restaurant had wireless and he was on his laptop, checking info on Los Angeles. He had decided to check into a hotel in downtown L.A. until he could figure out where to stay. He glanced out into the parking lot and noticed a police car parked behind his car. An officer was standing behind his car talking into a shoulder mike. He was looking at the Colorado plates on Roger's car. Not a good sign. Roger knew that if he ran those plates, they'd come back to that blue Corolla he had taken them from. Should he try to cook up a story, or just wait it out?

As he watched, another marked car pulled up beside the officer. The cop leaned in the window of the other car and they had a discussion. The new arrival pulled his unit into a parking place and he joined the other officer

252

behind Roger's car. They talked back and forth
and then headed for the entrance to the diner.

Roger shut off his laptop and stuffed it
into the backpack he used for a carrier. He left
some bills on the table and headed for the
restrooms. There was an exit by the restrooms,
but the door was marked as an emergency exit
only. He didn't want to sound an alarm, so he
turned around and headed back into the dining
area. At first, he didn't see the officers, then he
spotted them sitting in a booth with coffee in
front of them. He walked out through the door
without a glance in their direction. He headed
for his car. As he got near, he looked back in
the window of the diner. The cops were not in
view. They wouldn't be able to see him either.

Quickly, he tossed his laptop on the front
seat and got in the car. He started up and drove
out of the parking lot, taking care to avoid
passing by the window where the cops were
sitting. Once out of the parking area, he headed
into Barstow. He'd dump this car somewhere

quick. The description and plates would be known now. As soon as they discovered he'd left the parking lot, they'd have a description and the plates on the radio.

Roger stopped at a convenience store and asked directions to the bus station. He'd take a Greyhound bus into L.A. Safer that way.

CHAPTER 60

Roger parked in the bus station lot and entered the building. He found the schedules and saw that there were buses leaving for L.A. about every two or three hours. He bought a ticket for the next bus. It would take about four hours for the trip. It would let him off at the Los Angeles Downtown Station. He had no idea where that was and didn't want to attract attention by asking. He had an hour to kill.

He went to the bank of lockers and bought a key for one. He retuned to his car. He packed a few things in his backpack, along with his laptop. He had his shaving kit and a change of underwear in the backpack, and the cash in the gym bag. He put the backpack and the gym bag in the locker and the rest of his clothes in the trunk of the car. He could always buy new in L.A.

Roger drove the car to a strip mall a block away and parked it. Nobody would notice it there for a while anyway. Long enough for him to get out of town. He walked back to the bus station and retrieved his bags from the locker. He took a seat on a bench across from a Spanish family with two small children. The two kids, a boy and a girl were sleeping on the bench. The mother and father looked exhausted and were leaning against each other for support.

Roger sat on the bench, looking at the schedule and watching for any cops. The bus would be coming soon.

Roger looked at his last motel bill from a Best Western. He went to the payphone and called the 800 number listed on his receipt. The reservation clerk answered his call.

"Hello sir, how can I help you and for what city?"

"Los Angeles, something near the downtown area." Roger answered.

"We have the Dragon Gate Inn on north Hill Street. That is pretty near the city center."

"Give me the address and phone number, would you? I'll be arriving this afternoon, and I'd like to see if there are rooms available for a couple of days."

"Just a moment sir, and I'll see what's available." The clerk put him on hold with background music, interspersed with clicks. She came back on in less than a minute. She gave him the phone number and address.

"There are rooms available, shall I book you now?" She asked.

"No, I'll just stop in and check in when I get there, Thanks." Roger hung up before she could ask for a credit card. More than likely, they had plenty of rooms available. Now he would be set for a few days.

Just then, his bus was announced on the loudspeaker. He grabbed his two bags and went out to the loading area. He declined to have his bags put into the baggage compartment. He would carry them with him. He got on the bus and moved to the rear. He put his backpack on the shelf above the seat and put the gym bag with his money on the floor in front of his feet. He wanted it where he could keep an eye on it. There were some shifty looking characters riding the bus into L.A.

CHAPTER 61

It was a four-hour trip before the bus finally pulled into the Downtown Station in L.A. It took another five minutes to depart from the bus. He had his backpack over his shoulder and the gym bag in his hand. He'd find his hotel first, then shop for some more clothes. He'd worry about transportation after he'd surveyed the area and checked out some of the hangouts of the homeless.

He walked out of the bus station and went directly to a Bell Cab that was unloading a passenger.

"Take me to the Dragon Gate Inn on Hill Street." He told the cabbie. He took his backpack from his shoulder and got in the cab with his gym bag at his side.

"Sure 'ting." said the cab driver with a slight Spanish lilt.

He pulled out of the bus station and into the traffic. Roger watched as the city rolled by. Palm trees were situated along the streets. They came into Chinatown and he noticed they were on Hill Street. A short time later, the cab pulled into the Dragon Gate Inn. It was better than he expected. He paid the cab driver and walked towards the hotel. A pickup truck pulled in as the cab pulled out. Roger glanced at it, then went into the lobby. A pretty oriental woman was behind the counter. The lobby was nicely laid out with a gift shop and post office on his right. There was nobody waiting at the counter, so Roger walked up as the lady smiled at him.

"Good afternoon, sir. Do you have a reservation?" she asked.

"No, but I called your 800 number and they said you had rooms. Are there rooms still available."

"Yes, there are. Do you prefer smoking or non?

"Non smoking please, and one double bed will be fine. I'd like to pay cash up front for two nights, if I may."

"That is not necessary sir, you may just reserve it with your credit card."

"I'd rather pay cash." Roger said.

"Of course. Just fill in the registration card, if you would. Do you have any identification?"

Roger handed her the Fred Jackson drivers license and began filling out the form. He entered a false address on Lombard Street in San Francisco, and added a phone number with a "415" area code.

The girl entered some information from his driver's license into her computer and handed him back the license and two card keys for his room.

"Two nights in advance will be two hundred and fifty four dollars. That includes your phone deposit and the taxes on the room"

Roger counted out the money from his billfold. "I probably won't be using the phone." He said.

"In that case, your deposit will be returned upon check-out." The girl smiled at him.

"Fine." Roger smiled back at her.

"You are in room 315 Mr. Jackson." She turned the registration over and showed him a map of the hotel with room numbers. "We are here, and here is your room." She moved her finger from the card and pointed across the way.

Roger said his thanks and picked up his gym bag. His room was across the little courtyard outside of the lobby. He would walk across the parking and go up the outside stairway. That would be the shortest route. He wanted to take a shower and get some new clothes. He felt sweaty and grimy after the long bus ride.

CHAPTER 62

Roger hitched the backpack up on his shoulder and shifted the gym bag to his right hand. As he walked past the pickup parked by the curb, a man got out carrying a shopping bag. When he saw Roger, he dropped the bag and stepped forward.

"Richard!" he yelled.

Gary Frost! Roger froze for a second then took off running across the courtyard; Gary wasn't twenty feet behind him.

Roger pounded up the stairway, glancing back as he ran. Gary was closing in fast. At the top of the stairs, Roger turned around quickly and swung the gym bag at Gary's head. As it connected, Gary reflexively grabbed the bag and as he tripped backwards down the stairs he pulled the bag from Roger's grip.

Roger watched as he fell. Gary's eyes were on him. Gary landed in a heap at the bottom of the stairs, but he didn't appear to be seriously injured. He shook his head and pulled himself to his feet. He started back up the stairs.

"Stop! Police! You are under arrest!" Gary shouted at him, anger twisting his features. As he started up the stairway, his right leg gave out from under him. Gary grimaced with pain and leaned against the railing.

Roger waited no longer. He took off at a run through an opening between the rooms. On the other side, he found a stairway going down. He ran down the stairs and through a gate to the street. Traffic was fairly light, so he ran across the street and kept running until he was out of breath. He looked back over his shoulder. There was no sign of pursuit. He looked wildly around for a cab. A Checker cab was coming towards him, heading back towards the hotel. He stepped out in the street and waved it down. The cab pulled to a stop beside him.

"Take me to the bus depot" Roger panted at the driver, "I'm running late and I don't want to miss my bus. Please hurry!"

"You got it boss." the cabbie said as he reached over to start his meter. "Hop in the back."

Roger flung open the door and dropped his backpack on the seat next to him. The driver was on the move before he had the door completely shut. He pushed himself back in the seat and as low as he could as they passed the Dragon Gate. Just before he dropped below window level, he got a glimpse of Gary standing in the drive, the gym bag still in his hand. He was supporting himself by leaning against the wall, his right foot held off of the ground. He was looking right and left, and didn't notice the cab as it went by.

CHAPTER 63

Roger took out his billfold. He had exactly ninety-seven dollars and a little change. He needed to get to his stash in Las Vegas, and fast. Even more important, he had to get out of Los Angeles before Gary could shut down his escape.

The cab glided to a stop in front of the bus station. Roger had been watching the meter and had the money in his hand. He dropped it on the seat beside the driver and jumped out with a muttered, "Thanks" to the driver.

The driver looked down at the exact fare with no tip, "Yeah, man, you too. Have a nice day sucker." The tires chirped as he took off.

Roger ran into the station, looking wildly around for a schedule. He found a listing behind the ticket counter. Buses left regularly for Las Vegas. He got in the shortest line at the counter and fidgeted until it was his turn.

"One way to Vegas," he told the cashier. "Next bus too, please."

The man was counting some bills into his cash drawer. He looked up, irritated, "Just a minute sir." He kept counting the bills into the drawer. After what seemed an eternity, he looked up at Roger. "Vegas, you say?"

"Yes, the next one leaving, please."

"Did you say, 'one way' sir?"

"Yes, yes, one way." Roger was sweating, beads of it standing out on his forehead.

"I've got one that leaves in ten minutes. That soon enough for you?" The clerk was looking at his computer screen."

"That would be just fine," Roger replied, wiping his forehead with the back of his hand. "How much?"

"Forty dollars, one way. Your bus leaves at three thirty at gate 5."

Roger dug out his billfold and laid two twenties on the counter. The clerk took the money and handed Roger his ticket. "Gate 5 is right over there, on your left."

Roger stopped at the vending machines and got a ham and cheese sandwich and a bottle of water. That would have to last him until he got to Vegas. He hurried over and stood by the gate, watching the doors to the station, expecting the police to come barging in with guns drawn.

Ten minutes later, the bus began boarding. Roger was the first passenger on. He took a seat near the front of the bus, so that he could see if any pursuit was coming. After what seemed like an eternity, the bus began moving.

270

Roger slumped down in his seat, peering cautiously out the window. No sign of any police cars. He looked at his ticket; they would be stopping at the Amtrak station before they left L.A. He wasn't clear yet. There weren't any layovers, but there were stops in El Monte, Claremont and Barstow before they got to Las Vegas at nine thirty that evening. Roger had a long, long six hours ahead of him.

After the bus left El Monte, Roger began to relax a little. He took a drink of his water. His stomach hadn't settled enough to try to tackle the stale sandwich yet. By the time they reached Barstow, Roger had finished his sandwich and trying to figure out his next move. First, of course, he had to get his money out of his storage unit. He had rented that under the Fred Jackson name. He'd abandon that as soon as he got his money out. He had around $80,000 in cash there. He'd have to leave Vegas too. They could track him there with the Fred Jackson name. He wished he had another identity to use. He still had his Richard

Whiteman identification in his backpack, maybe he could use that until he found something new. It probably wouldn't be much safer, but he didn't have many alternatives. His mother would have some saying like, "Look on the bright side of things." Problem was, he couldn't see a bright side.

CHAPTER 64

Gary pushed himself off of the wall and limped into the hotel office. The girl behind the counter stared at him, the color drained out of her face. She had witnessed the scene with Roger.

"Call the police." Gary told her, wincing with pain as he moved to the desk. "It's an emergency." He set the gym bag on the counter and put his weight on his arms as he leaned over. He ran a hand over his face.

What the hell was Richard, no, Roger, doing in L.A.?

The girl behind the counter held the phone out to Gary, "I have the police on the line."

Gary tried to explain the situation to the dispatcher over the phone, stressing the urgency of the situation, that he had just seen a murder suspect and a man that was on the FBI's wanted list. The dispatcher was not impressed. "I'll have a car there very shortly, you can explain it all to them." The line went dead.

Great. Gary thought, by the time I can get this cleared up, Roger Wardlow will have done his disappearing act again.

"Can I please see the registration for that man that just checked in?" he asked the girl behind the counter. She was still pale and her hands shook as she pushed the card across the counter.

Fred Jackson, San Francisco, was the name on the card. *Something else to check out*, Gary thought. *I wonder if he's got any more names to use.*

With that thought in mind, Gary opened the gym bag. There were some papers on top, and an old Medford Mail Tribune lying neatly under them. Gary lifted the Tribune up by a corner and saw the stacks of bills underneath.

Time to call the feebies.

Gary pulled his cell phone from his belt and dialed Ramirez number from memory.

"FBI, Ramirez."

"Hi Rich, Gary Frost here, I've got some news for you."

"Hey Frosty. How's it hangin' man?" Rich was evidently glad to hear from him.

"I've just run into Roger Wardlow. Lucky bastard got away again, but he left behind some cash you might be interested in."

"Give me your location and don't move. I'll have an agent there post haste."

Gary told him where he was and that he had tried to get the LAPD moving without luck.

"Never mind that, I'll call the office there, it's out on Wilshire, they'll be there shortly. They'll contact the PD too. I hope we're not too late to catch Wardlow."

275

"He might be using the name Fred Jackson. That's how he registered here at the hotel. Who knows what other names he's got available. Don't think he'd be using the Richard Whiteman ID, but you never know. Check them both out, will you?" Gary was fingering the papers; they were mostly Richard Whiteman's or papers that Wardlow had accumulated while using the Whiteman ID.

"I've got the field office on the line. Anything else you want to pass on?" Ramirez was talking to both Gary and the field office at the same time. "They say the field office on Wilshire is probably the closest office time wise to your location. They have two agents heading your way."

"Nothing yet, I'll hang onto this gym bag with the money in it until your men get here. See if they can get the LAPD to start checking all the terminals and cabs. Probably too late now. Wardlow moves fast when he has to."

"Done. Hey, thanks for the tip. I owe you one, big time. Call me later and fill me in on what's happening, o.k?"

"You got it Rich. I'll be in touch later today." Ramirez gave Gary his cell phone number and thanked him again before signing off.

Gary sat down in one of the comfortable chairs in the lobby. He put his head back and closed his eyes. What a way to start back to work. He had checked into the hotel only an hour before Wardlow had come in. They could have been staying in the same place and never run into each other. Out of all the hotels in Los Angeles, fate had certainly played a hand in this choice.

CHAPTER 65

Roger caught a cab at the bus terminal and had him wait at the storage facility while he picked up the suitcase with his money in it. He took a bundle of hundreds and another of twenties from the case and stuck them in his inside pocket of his windbreaker. He took the padlock too. He didn't bother to close out the account. There was still time left on the lease, but he wasn't about to try to get a deposit back.

He had the cab driver drop him at a small motel near the airport. It was getting late now, and he was exhausted. He rented a room for the night, putting a phony name and address on the registration and paying cash in advance. He took the suitcase full of cash and his backpack to his room. He'd think clearer in the morning.

He wanted to get to Reno. The bus took a round about route through Utah and the trip was 19 hours long. Cabs and limos were too expensive. They'd raise flags just because of the unusual fee. He could get an America West flight direct to Reno, but he couldn't take the suitcase full of money on the plane, either as carryon or checked. Security would check it either way and he'd be up a creek when they found all that money.

He could call ahead and get a reservation at the Sands in Reno, then Fed-Ex the money to the hotel. That would be the best. He'd use the Richard Whiteman credit card for the reservation and flight and hope there weren't any flags on them. He didn't see any other way.

He would wait until morning. He wanted to have a clear head when he did this. If it took an extra day in Vegas, so be it.

CHAPTER 66

Gary sat in the chair in his room at the Dragon Gate. His ankle had swollen and was dark blue and black, at least a sprain. He had been soaking it in the wastebasket with ice and cold water. The two agents sat across from him on a sofa, jackets off, badges and pistols at their waists, notebooks in hand. They had a folder lying between them. It contained the information they had on the Roger Wardlow case.

They looked like kids to Gary. Tom, the leader of the two, was blonde and looked like a California surfer. Charlie was his complete opposite, dark and swarthy. His real name was Carlos, but Tom had introduced him as Charlie, and that's what he preferred, evidently. Tom was running the discussion, and starting to piss Gary off.

"So, after you let Wardlow get away, why did it take fifteen minutes to get LAPD involved." He smirked, trying to let Gary know that the remark about Wardlow getting away was supposed to be his idea of a joke.

"Like I told you when the patrol car was here, the dispatcher didn't take me serious, wanted the patrolmen to make the call. I haven't checked into my new outfit yet, so I don't even have a badge to back me up."

Gary had given them all the info he had, and had added some ideas on Wardlow's whereabouts. They had their own.

"Wardlow came to Oregon from Nevada. He had spent some time there, mostly in Las Vegas. I'd check that out first. I don't think he could have gone very far, he may still be trying to get connections out of town."

"Nah, he's headed to Mexico. He knows that the FBI is on his trail by now; he'll want to get out of the country. We'll give Mexico, probably Tijuana, priority, then we'll put Las Vegas on a lookout too." Tom flipped his notebook closed and stood, Charlie following his example. They picked up their jackets from the chair they had dropped them on.

"Don't bother to get up, we'll find our way out," Tom smirked again as he opened the door. "Ramirez said to keep you in the loop, so we'll contact you if anything comes up. I've got your cell, but when you get set in your new office, give me a call to update your contact info."

Gary raised a hand as they left. There had been a frenzy of activity when the patrolmen had finally arrived, followed shortly by the FBI agents. After the confusion had settled down and Gary had explained the situation, the LAPD cops had called their office and Tom had talked to their commander giving him instructions to watch all the airline, train and bus terminals and to put out a bulletin. They wouldn't have a picture to go with it yet, just the description and the names that Roger had used in the past.

Gary had no great expectations. By the time the info had been dispersed, it was nearly four o'clock. A bad time, as it was shift change for a lot of the terminals, as well as the police. Information would have to be passed from one shift to another, and Gary had experience with that in the past. A lot was lost during that transition. In actuality, Roger was already on the bus and between the Amtrak station in Los Angeles, and El Monte at the time the information was being relayed.

He looked at his ankle again. He'd have to check into an ER and get it looked at. If it was broken, he might be late reporting to his new job. A great way to start off his return to duty.

CHAPTER 67

Roger sat at his laptop, bleary eyed. He had slept poorly, waking at every door slam and arrival of the late night guests. The sun was starting to edge into the room. He was logged into Expedia on the internet, reserving a flight to Reno on America West. He made the reservation in the name of D. Whitman, deliberately misspelling the name. He used Richard's credit card to confirm the reservation. If they had Richard Whiteman flagged, he might get away with it. He wasn't sure about the credit card, but it was accepted and he had a reservation for that afternoon. He had done the same with the Sand's hotel in Reno and had a room reserved for the next two days. He had gone for the package and had the flight, the room and a rental car set up. He would be a nervous wreck until everything worked, if it did.

He had made coffee in the room and sat sipping the vile tasting stuff while he worked. He shut down the laptop and put it back in the backpack. He exchanged the Fred Jackson driver's license for Richard's and stuck the credit card in his billfold with it. He took a quick shower and shaved. He put on the clean underwear from his backpack and threw the old in the trash. His shirt and pants were wrinkled and dirty, but they'd be o.k. for short while longer. The windbreaker was a dark blue and looked o.k. The cash was still safe in the inside pocket.

He walked next door to a small café and had breakfast. He felt much better after he had eaten. Now he had to take care of the cash. He walked back to the motel and had them call him a cab. He retrieved his suitcase and backpack from his room and checked out of the motel.

The cab arrived shortly and he got in the back and turned to the driver. "Do you know where there is a place that will ship packages?"

"Sure, there's a UPS store in a strip mall back towards town." The driver was looking at him in the rear view mirror.

"Let's go there first, I've got a couple of stops to make, that o.k. with you?" Roger met his gaze in the mirror.

"O.K. with me, you'll have to pay for the time."

"Fine with me, let's go."

Roger sat back in the cab as they took off. It was a short trip, less than a mile from the motel. The UPS store was located in a small strip mall along with a coffee shop, a dentist office and a few other stores.

"Wait here, I'll be right back." Roger grabbed the suitcase and walked into the package store. He was the only customer. He walked up to the counter and placed the suitcase on top.

"Good morning, how can I help you?" the young man asked. He was dark skinned and looked to be a Pakistani, or Indian. His diction was flawless and his smile full of bright white teeth.

"I'd like to send some things up to Reno. Can you pack this in a box and overnight it for me?" Roger pushed the suitcase towards him.

"I could just put a label on the outside, if you'd like. Save you a little doing it that way."

"No, I need to have it packed inside another box. The locks aren't too good." Roger lay the suitcase on it's side.

"Sure, whatever you want. Just fill out this sheet with the destination address. It will go out this morning, probably be in Reno early tomorrow morning."

Roger pulled the paper towards him and put in the Richard Whiteman name, the Sands address from his itinerary and handed it back to the clerk.

"Can you put a 'Hold for Arrival' on the box by the address?"

The clerk was already putting the suitcase in a large box, with some packing around the sides.

"Sure, I'll use a marker and put it in big letters so they can't miss it." He checked the sheet that Roger had filled out. He had put clothing down as the contents.

"Do you want insurance on this?"

"No, just be sure to overnight it." Roger watched as the clerk put the box, now sealed, on the scale. If it was lost, he wasn't going to be able to collect any insurance anyway.

"Twenty three dollars and fifty seven cents. Be there tomorrow morning. There is a tracking number here on your receipt."

Roger watched as the young man affixed the label and postage. His future was in that box. He handed over two twenties and took his change. He left the smiling clerk and returned to the cab.

"Can you find me a Wal-Mart?" he asked the cabbie.

The driver put down the paper he had been reading and checked Roger out in the rearview mirror again.

"Sure, you want me to wait there too? It's costing you, you know?"

"Yes, It won't take me long." Roger sat back in the seat and put the backpack on the floorboards as they took off. One more stop and then the tests would begin with the airline, car rental and hotel.

It was a longer drive this time. Roger didn't mind, he had several hours to kill before he had to be at the airport. The driver pulled up in front of the Wal Mart and let Roger out.

"I'll be parked right over there when you come out, with the meter running." The driver pointed as Roger got out.

"Fine, I'm leaving my backpack in the cab. Be back shortly."

Roger closed the door and entered the store; he had a flashback when he saw the man who was the greeter. He had looked like Richard for a second.

He bought a pair of chino's and a shirt. He'd change at the airport and dump his old clothes. He'd pick up more clothes once he got to Reno. He was back at the cab in less than ten minutes.

"That was quick," said the driver, putting his paper down once again, "Where to now?"

"McCarren airport. That's my last stop." Roger sat back in the seat, putting the package from Wal Mart on the seat beside him.

The driver took off without a word. They pulled up to the airport and Roger paid him off, giving him an extra ten.

"Thanks man, have a good trip." The driver smiled at Roger, finally turning around in the seat.

Roger got his package and backpack and entered the airport. He had plenty of time before his flight. He looked around until he found a Men's room. He found an empty stall and quickly changed clothes. He put his old clothes in the Wal Mart sack and dumped them in the trash as he left.

Roger stopped in a coffee shop and killed some time over coffee. He was too nervous for food. The coffee wasn't helping his nerves either, so he went to one of the many rows of slot machines and played the machines for another hour, losing sixty dollars while he did.

Finally, he couldn't wait any more. He got in line at the ticket counter for America West. He looked around to see if there were any cops looking for him. There were no uniforms by the counter, but there were security people all over the airport anyway.

His turn came up. He walked shakily to the counter and put Richard's driver's license on it.

"I have a reservation to Reno." Richard watched as the clerk picked up the license. "Flight 530, leaving at twelve thirty."

The clerk barely looked at him, "I'm sorry sir, I don't see a reservation under your name."

"Could you check again? I made the reservation through Expedia this morning."

Roger watched as she continued to look at the screen.

"Oh, wait a minute, Here's one from Expedia with the name 'Whitman', it must have been a typo, happens a lot. D. Whitman, made this morning about seven, that sound right?" She looked up at Roger, a slight smile on her face.

"Damn, I should have waited until I had my coffee this morning. Everybody calls me Dick, I probably put D for Dick and missed the 'e' in my hurry. I was kind of rushed this morning." He watched her for any sudden change of expression that would show him as being flagged.

The smile didn't alter. "Happens. I'll just change it here. Do you have that credit card with you?"

Roger slid the credit card across the counter. The clerk picked it up and glanced from it to the screen. "Yep, that's the one, the numbers match."

292

"Any bags to check?" She slid the credit card and license back to Roger.

"No, no bags." Roger felt weak with relief. It had worked!

He had bought a round trip ticket. It would be less suspicious and he sure wasn't worried about the expense. He took the ticket the girl handed him.

"Gate A-15, you probably should head on up through security now, you want to be at the gate shortly."

Roger smiled at her and headed for the line for security. The worse test was over. Now just the car rental and the hotel. At least he could get to Reno.

CHAPTER 68

The flight to Reno was short. Roger got off of the plane at the Reno-Tahoe International airport halfway expecting to be met by a bunch of cops. Didn't happen. He went to the Avis rental counter, checking behind him and around the counter, but there wasn't anything that raised his suspicion.

He went through the same routing with the clerk at Avis. More smiles, with him acting contrite for making such a stupid mistake. He got the keys to his car, a Ford Taurus, and rode the shuttle to the parking area. The shuttle dropped him off and he put his backpack in the seat next to him and drove out of the lot. One more test to go, this would be the important one.

He parked in the lot at the Sands and took his backpack with him to the desk at the hotel. There was a line with a velvet rope marking off the waiting area. Roger got in line and waited his turn. The line went fast, there were five clerks working the check in.

"Name sir?" the young man behind the counter asked Roger.

Roger explained up front that there had been a mistake in his reservation and told him what to look for. The clerk went right to the reservation and made the necessary changes. He was in!

"I have a package being Fed-Exed to me here. It should arrive tomorrow morning. Would you please give me a call when it arrives?"

"Of course sir, we'll notify you right away." The clerk smiled at Roger and handed him his room key. "Do you need any help with bags?"

"Thank you, no. I'll be fine." Roger smiled back. *Little did he know how fine.*

Roger went to his room and laid his backpack on the bed. Time to get some traveling clothes. He would get his suitcase of money in the morning and get out of here. He had been unbelievably lucky so far. Fate taking him on another ride, uphill this time.

.

CHAPTER 69

Gary was back in his room at the Dragon Gate. He had a bad sprain, no broken bones. He had checked in at his new office, hobbling with a cane. His new boss, Don Winslow, had heard about the run in with Roger and his eyes sparkled as he grinned at Gary.

"Couldn't even wait to get on the clock, could you?" He was impressed with the good reference that Rich Ramirez had given Gary.

Gary grinned back, "I wish Wardlow had waited. I would have been a lot more effective with a badge and gun. Might have even stopped him."

"You'll get plenty more chances now that you're back in L.A. Don't let it get you down. "With that ankle, you'll probably be driving a desk the first few days. That might be good. You can review some of the cases you'll be working on. When you come in Monday, I'll introduce you around and get you teamed up. You're going to like it here."

After his warm welcome at LAPD, he hadn't felt quite so bad about the run in with Roger. Now he had been thinking about it again. He decided to call Donna back in Shady Glen and bring her up to date.

'Hello," Donna answered on the second ring.

"You must have been right by the phone." Gary grinned at the sound of her voice. She sounded good.

"Gary! How are you? What's going on?"

"I'm fine, just wanted to let you know I saw Richard dash Roger today."

"What? You did? Where?"

"It's almost funny," Gary said, "We were checked in at the same hotel in Los Angeles. I saw him in the parking. I gave chase on foot, and when I got near to grabbing him, he bonked me with about a hundred grand in cash in a gym bag, and got away. I got the gym bag though."

"You don't say. Crazy. And Gary, uh, how did he look?"

From the sound of her voice, Gary knew that Donna still had feelings for Richard/Roger. She had taken the news the hardest.

"You know what Donna? He really looked pretty good, before I scared him half to death anyway. I was surprised, I was really glad to see him at first. Not because he's a fugitive, but because we were friends at one time. I kind of miss the old fart."

"Yeah, me too. I still find it hard to believe what all he did. It must have been something temporary, he was a good man at heart, I know he was." Donna's voice was quiet, and Gary could hear the tears over the phone line.

"I tend to agree Donna. I know I shouldn't, being a lawman and all, but I kind of hope he gets away. Maybe he can find an identity that he can live with."

CHAPTER 70

If everything worked out, he wouldn't be staying in Sparks long. Roger's package arrived the following morning, just as promised. He had put the package in the trunk of the Taurus and checked out of the Sands. Now he could get away from the Richard Whiteman identity again. Chances are they could track him to Reno from his trail as D. Whitman. The credit card number would be the first to raise flags. If he hadn't been traveling on a weekend, it probably would have raised them before now. He had checked into a Super 8 in Sparks, which was sort of a suburb of Reno on the east.

Roger drove around Sparks until he found what he was looking for. It was a pickup with a camper on it. It had a "For Sale" sign in the window, and was parked by a building that had rooms for rent by the day, week, or month.

If he guessed right, it belong to some gambler who was down on his luck.

He walked around the truck, checking the tires and overall condition. It didn't look too bad. The tires were good, and although the setup was several years old, it looked well taken care of. Instead of a phone number on the sign, there was a room number. Roger assumed it was for a room in the building it was parked in front of. He walked over to the entrance and looked at the rows of mailboxes with numbers painted on them. Some of the boxes had names, others didn't. Number 17 was in the third row of boxes. There was no name on it. Roger checked the layout of the rooms. There was an interior courtyard, with small rooms leading out to the center. A swimming pool had been filled up with dirt and had a broken down swing set on it. The place looked like an old motel that had gone to seed, and probably was.

He walked down to room 17 and knocked on the door. There was no response, but the TV was blaring through the closed door. He knocked louder, and the lock clicked back.

The face that looked out at him was a wreck. Bloodshot eyes, three days of beard and a breath that could peel paint. He appeared about fifty, but could have been twenty years older or younger, it was hard to tell.

"Whadduwant?" he mumbled, another blast of alcoholic breath following the words.

"You own the pickup camper?" Roger asked, squinting with the sunlight and odors.

The eyes took on a sharper look, blinking away some of the stupor. "Yep, sure do. You interested?"

"Might be, depends on what you're asking" Roger felt he had what he wanted here.

"I've been askin five g's for it, but I'd take forty five hunnert cash." The eyes now took on a scheming look. "It's in really good shape, runs great."

"How about a test run," Roger wanted to be sure he wasn't buying a pile of junk; he wouldn't have much recourse if he did.

"Sure, lemme get my boots on." The man stumbled back into the room, leaving the door open. Roger wasn't about to follow him in, the room was a pigsty. The man was right back, boots on and keys in his hand. "Foller me, I'll give you the tour."

Roger followed him back out front to where the pickup was parked. The skinny man in the t-shirt walked to the back and stuck a key in the camper door. He opened the door and stepped up into the camper. Roger followed him in.

The interior was much neater than he expected. It was much, much more compact than his trailer had been. There was an unmade bed that went over the top of the pickup. Other than that, it was surprisingly clean. There was the same utilization of space that was in his camper. No room wasted anywhere. There was a small dinette, small two-burner stove and tiny refrigerator. A small sink was next to the stove.

"Here 'tis," the man waved a hand at the interior. "Everthin is automatic, runs on gas, AC or battery, depending on what you got hooked up. It's got a twenty gallon fresh water tank, and I bought one a them there outdoor showers that hooks on the back with a curtain. It's got it's own little water tank and stores in the outside compartment. Camper comes complete with jacks and an inverter and converter. That means you either get 12 volts when you're plugged into an AC outlet, or 110 volts off'n your battery if you need it."

Roger was impressed. It wasn't ideal, but it would work. He could live out of this for months if he had to. "How about the truck, what shape's it in?"

"Let's take her for a spin, I'll show you." They got back out of the camper. He closed and locked the camper door and walked around to the driver's side door. "I'll drive first, show you what's what, then you can take it over, get a feel for it."

Roger got in on the passenger side. There were two jump seats in the back. The truck was a big F-150 Ford that had a solid feel to it.

"Got the big V-8 and heavy duty suspension. Got a transmission cooler and heavy-duty alternator. This baby was designed to carry a camper."

Roger was impressed with how clean the truck was. Compared to the owner, the truck was in much better shape.

"Haven't had it out much, I've been out of work. I used to work construction, traveled from site to site. Had a bad run of luck here in Sparks, got some of my tools in hock. I need to sell the truck to get back to work."

They drove down the street, then pulled up on the interstate and ran up to 65 mph. The truck was solid and steady. Roger was surprised at the acceleration. They drove to the next exit and he pulled off and stopped at the bottom of the ramp.

"I'll pull around the corner, then you can take the wheel." The skinny man checked the traffic then pulled around and stopped. He got out of the truck and walked around the to the passenger side, Roger trading places with him.

They strapped in and Roger took off. The truck handled well. It was much heavier and handled a lot different than either the Explorer or the Camry. It was really easier to drive than the Explorer with the trailer. He drove around the city for a while then headed back up to the interstate. Skinny gave him directions back to the room.

"Whadda ya think?" Skinny asked. The hope in his eyes was almost pathetic. "Great setup, huh?"

"Not bad," Roger said, stroking his chin. "Price is a little steep though."

Skinny had the scheming look back in his eyes. "Forty five hunnert has to be my bottom price. I'm gonna have to get me another pickup and get my tools outta hock, can't let it go for less."

"Tell you what," Roger was starting to enjoy this, "I'm in a hurry to get out of town and back on the road, I'll give you four grand cash money and drive it off as is. I'll send you the plates back when I get home and get it registered. You got the title?"

Skinny was trying hard not to look pleased. "Gee, I dunno, Yeah, I got the title, but is that legal? I mean keepin' the plates?" He scratched his scrawny belly, "That's not goin to be enough cash for me either, I mean, I gotta get my tools an' another truck."

"O.K., sorry, I guess I'll have to look around some more." Roger turned to walk away.

"Whoa. Wait. If'n you got the cash on you, I guess we can deal." Skinny was holding Rogers sleeve in his hand.

Roger stopped and looked down at the hand on his sleeve. Skinny dropped his arm and took a step back. "Sorry, didn't mean to grab at you like that."

Roger smiled at the pathetic creature standing there. "No harm done, let's deal."

Skinny broke into a big smile, "Yur on, partner."

CHAPTER 71

Roger had Skinny, whose real name turned out to be Dave, drive the camper over to the Super 8 and leave it in the parking lot. They had closed the deal, exchanging cash for title and Roger took him back to his rooming house in the rental car, leaving him at the curb with a big grin on his face. He'd probably be back in the casino within an hour, broke again in two. Roger drove the Taurus back to the motel and moved his bags into the camper. He left the Taurus where it was, got in the camper and headed east on interstate 80.

CHAPTER 72

Bars were a good place to hunt. Roger knew just what he wanted, another identity, just like Richard. No relatives, no ties, some loner about his own age and description. It wasn't as easy as Roger had thought. First, he had to find someone that looked enough like him to pass a cursory examination. That was proving difficult. He found two in the past week, hundreds of miles apart. The first was a family man; he had just stopped in for a drink after a meeting. The second was married, and a councilman in the town.

Roger drifted from town to town, searching for his new life. The days turned into another week. It had to be perfect or it wouldn't work. He would stop into a bar and stick around for an hour or two, keeping his drinks to a minimum. He found that most of the bars in the towns were hangouts for the regulars. He started picking bars that were on the edge of town, or close to motels, the seedier the better. Parking was easier to find too, the camper wasn't that easy to find parking for in the downtown areas.

He had been at it for over a month now, searching for the perfect subject. He was starting to get discouraged. Time was against him. It had been so easy the first time with Richard. He had checked the Des Moines Register on his laptop computer when he was in Rapid City. The search for him was back on. He had found a short article stating that the F.B.I. had new information and expected an arrest soon.

CHAPTER 73

He was in a bar in South Dakota, west of Rapid City, just outside of Sturgis. The bar he was in was close to a run down motel and was half filled with patrons. It had appeared to have promise, and Roger had been coming every night for the last three days. Most of the people tonight were men, and there were a couple of them that looked like they might work. One of them had a short beard and was wearing a leather vest with a Harley Davidson emblem on the back. He was shooting pool with another man, who looked like a local, who was dressed in jeans and boots and wore a cowboy hat.

The other was sitting across the bar from him. He was dressed in a wrinkled suit, with a tie loosely knotted at the neck. The top button of his shirt was open and he looked exhausted. He looked up every time someone came in the bar, and then took another gulp from the drink in front of him. He was sitting alone in the shadows and it was difficult to see his features. The build looked about right.

Roger and the man across the bar were both watching the TV screen. The sound was off, it couldn't be heard over the jukebox anyway. The closed caption was scrolling down the screen. There was a story on the local channel about a bloody homicide in Rapid City that day. A man, Glen Davis, had come home unexpectedly and caught his wife and boyfriend together. He had killed them both with a large knife, stabbing them both over twenty times each. According to the police, he was still at large. There were more details that would be on the ten o'clock news. There were a couple of armed robberies at convenience stores, one of which had a surveillance camera photo of the robber that could have been anybody. After that announcement, they switched to the weather. A heavy rain was expected tonight with clearing in the early hours. A sunny day was predicted for tomorrow.

Roger had been carrying the Richard Whiteman ID in his billfold, thinking it would be better than the expired drivers license of Fred Jackson. After tonight, he'd switch and get rid of Richard's papers. He knew that if they were looking for him as Roger Wardlow, they would be looking for him as Richard Whiteman too. If he were lucky, he'd have a new ID tonight.

Roger picked up his drink and wandered around the bar. He stopped by the jukebox, then past the pool table. He kept on until he was on the same side of the bar as the stranger.

Roger climbed up on the stool next to him and smiled at him.

"Hi, stranger, my name's Dick, what's yours?"

The man looked up startled and stared back at Roger. He appeared nervous and on edge for some reason, must have had a bad day. After sitting motionless for a moment, the man picked up his drink.

"The name's Bob." He said, then took a gulp of his drink. He turned back to the bar and TV screen.

"You from around here, Bob? Don't think I've seen you in here before." The man had a striking resemblance to Roger, about the same age; slightly overweight, same color eyes and graying. His hair was a little longer than Roger's, otherwise, they could have been brothers. Maybe, just maybe, the hunt was over.

"N-no, he stammered, I'm ah, from Chicago, yeah, Chicago. Just passing through."

Roger was struck with the coincidence. Bob, same name he had chosen when he first met Richard Whiteman, "just passing through", the same phrase. Maybe fate was telling him something. He decided he would see where this would go.

"Yeah, me too, passing through, that is. I've been here a week, time to move on. I've been thinking about heading down towards

316

Denver. That's one of the perks of being alone and unemployed, no obligations to anybody."

Bob turned back towards Roger. He had his attention now. He was probably bored with this part of the country, being from Chicago and all. No big buildings here and a little less exciting too.

"What brings you out here to the Black Hills Bob? Long way from Chicago."

Bob paused, then leaning a little towards Roger, said, "I've been making customer calls. I'm uh, I'm a salesman." Bob stammered a little, he'd probably had more than a couple of drinks. His eyes were blood shot and he needed a shave.

"What you selling Bob, out here in the middle of nowhere?"

Bob paused again, "I'm... ah selling business machines to small businesses." He glanced around the bar, then back at Roger. "You retired? Or just out of work?"

317

"A little of both," Roger replied, "Got a little nest egg, more of a separation package, got terminated with a reduction in force from my job at a finance company. Not quite old enough to draw my pension yet."

Another customer came in the bar. He took off his cowboy hat and shook the water from it. It had started raining. Bob had snapped his head back towards the door when he came in. Now he leaned back into the shadows again. He picked up his glass and drained it.

Roger motioned with two fingers at the bartender, who nodded and began filling their drinks. "Looks like it's getting nasty out, might as well have another. I'll buy this round." Bob didn't argue, just toasted Roger with his glass and took another big gulp.

"Thanks."

They had several more, the drinks seeming to have no effect whatever on Bob, but Roger was getting a little woozy. He'd have to be careful. He had managed to find out a little more about Bob. It was like pulling teeth to get anything out of him. He was alone and unmarried. According to him, he had a sister in Chicago that was married and had a family. They weren't close. They had a big fight when their parents died and hadn't spoken since.

"Think I'll have a coffee and hit the road," Roger said. "Traffic should be light tonight, with the rain and all. How about you, Bob? Drop you off somewhere?"

"Thanks, I'd appreciate that. I'm staying at that motel down the street. I walked down and it's just far enough to get soaked in this rain." Bob knocked back the last of his drink.

They both had coffee black and left the bar together. Roger had parked the camper at the far end of the lot, just in case he had to bring somebody back to it. He wanted to be out of sight of the bar. The jack handle was under the seat on the driver's side where he could reach it quickly. He had taped the handle for a better grip. He was prepared. A plastic drop cloth was in the back, ready to roll his victim in. He was going to get his new identity tonight. There would be no sloppy mistakes again.

Roger had his keys out as they approached the camper. He unlocked the driver's door then opened it. He looked back at Bob. Bob was looking back towards the bar; he had no clue what was coming. Roger turned back and had his hand on the jack handle. He got a good grip on it, and turned back to Bob.

Bob was facing him now. Instead of an easy victim, Roger was now facing a man armed with a large hunting knife. The knife was low and pointed at him. He swung the jack handle. Bob easily stepped inside of Roger's swing and brought the knife up hard, driving it deep into Roger's chest. He yanked the knife out and stepped back. Roger dropped the jack handle and put his hand over the hole in his chest. Blood was running out everywhere, mixing with the rainwater on the blacktop of the parking lot.

He slowly fell to the ground, feeling the life run out of his chest.

Bob reached over and took the keys out of the door. He dragged Roger to the back of the camper. He got Roger's billfold and stuck it in his jacket pocket. He tried keys until he found the one that opened the door to the camper. He pulled the door open and was surprised to see the folded tarp on the floor. He quickly spread it out and rolled Roger into it. He bundled him into the back of the camper headfirst, then slammed the door and locked it. He'd dispose of the body later.

Glen Davis took the drivers license from the billfold and looked at the likeness on it. Close enough. No more Glen Davis. From now on, he was Richard Whiteman, a free man! He ran up to the cab of the pickup and pulled out of the parking lot, turning on the lights as he headed towards the interstate.

In the back of the camper, wrapped in the tarp, Roger was feeling cold. He knew he was dying. He had come so close. Odd memories ran through his mind; all jumbled together. One in particular stood out. It was a memory of his mother, holding him by the shoulders when he was a child and looking into his eyes. His last thought was of her, passing on another gem of her wisdom. "Don't talk to strangers." She said, and faded into the gathering darkness.

The End

JERRY HOOTEN

Jerry was a U.S. Navy Electronics Specialist in a guided missile group for four years. He started in law enforcement in a small police department as a reserve officer and worked part time as a dispatcher and jailer for the county sheriff. He spent twenty-one years as a security specialist with the U.S. Postal Inspection Service installing covert surveillance equipment and physical security systems. He assisted in computer forensics and worked with other agencies and police departments to help in their investigations.

He served his last years with the Postal Service as the Area Security Coordinator for the Midwest Area.

He currently is a consultant to mystery writers, providing information on police procedures, weapons, surveillance techniques, and doing research in forensics.

He has assisted such great mystery writers as: Michael Connelly, Jim Swain, and the late Barbara Seranella. He has written and self-published his own mysteries, *Don't Talk to*

Strangers, the sequel, *Dead End* and several stand-alone novels, *Friends and Others,* a fantasy mystery, *Hunter,* a thriller, and *The Pension Plan.*
All of his books are available as digital books at Amazon, Barnes and Noble, Smashwords and other digital outlets.

He maintains two websites, one as a resource for mystery writers: www.jerryhooten.com Another for security and investigative information:
www.tech-conrite.com.

Credit and special thanks for the cover photo to Bob Modersohn, professional photographer and friend.
www.bobmodersohn.com

Proof

Made in the USA
Charleston, SC
14 August 2012